UNSPOKEN VALOR

STEVEN ABERNATHY

UNSPOKEN VALOR

STEVEN ABERNATHY

Mockingbird Lane Press

Unspoken Valor
Copyright © 2014 Steven Abernathy

Mockingbird Lane Press—Maynard, Arkansas

ISBN: 978-1-6341549-3-2

0 9 8 7 6 5 4 3 2 1

Library of Congress Control Number: 2014954454

Mockingbird Lane Press USA
Maynard, Arkansas
www.mockingbirdlanepress.com
Front cover design by John Abernathy
Back cover design by Jamie Johnson

Inspired by and dedicated to Jack Abernathy, devoted husband and father; church music director, businessman, and, least important to him, Airman in the United States Army Air Corps during World War II

Chapter 1

March, 2007

The day was perfect. The intense blue of the sky brought smiles and comments from all who looked upward into the heavens; the air was crisp but not cold, ideal for March. The wind co-operated just enough to make the new growth of grass rustle at the feet of all in attendance, and flags at the entrance waved in a majestic fashion, punctuating the solemnity of the occasion. It was a perfect day, except for the fact that the event was a funeral.

At least two hundred were in attendance at the graveside service. The men were solemn, dressed in everything from dark suits with polished black shoes to denim overalls and work boots. The women were much the same, their dress reflecting the solemn attire of the wealthy to the Sunday best of the poorest in town who wanted to pay their respects to a good man. Jack had been laid to rest in a dark gray suit from J.C. Penny, holding in his hands a church hymnal. He looked at peace, and he was.

The coffin was closed now, draped with an American flag. Jack was a veteran of World War II, but many in the small town were unaware of that fact because he never spoke of the war or his role in it.

Townsfolk had known him as a local businessman who had always treated them with fairness and compassion. He was also known as a devoted husband and father, a big supporter of the local school and as a Christian man who devoted much time to his church as volunteer music director for the last fifty years, an active deacon who took great interest in the operation of the church, and a hands-on Christian who was always there to visit the needy and hold out a hand to help whenever it was needed.

Some of the older folks remembered him going off to service during the war. A few even remembered that he had been wounded and spent time in a hospital before coming home, but most had little or no knowledge of Jack's service. Even his wife of almost sixty years and his grown children had little knowledge of his activities in the war. The most he would ever say when pressed with questions was, "That part of my life is in the past...I don't dwell on it...I don't even remember it."

Just before the service was to begin, two blue vans with United States Air Force insignias pulled into the cemetery. A group of young men dressed in Air Force uniforms emerged and began moving to an apparently prearranged staging area several yards away from the group of mourners. The funeral director met them at the designated spot, spoke briefly with the officer in charge of the honor guard, and returned to the small pulpit that had been placed at the head of the coffin for the service. As the Air Force honor guard was preparing for the service, onlookers noticed a bagpiper formally dressed in British Army honor guard attire, complete with kilt, sporin, ghillie brogues, and skean dhus, emerge from their official van, then walk to an area on the other side of the gravesite from the honor guard.

Whispers and looks of astonishment erupted within the group of mourners. "Who are these people?" seemed to be the question of the hour. "Is that a *real* military honor guard? Why are they here? And is that a *real* bagpiper? I've never seen one before, except on television!" World War II veterans were dying at a rapid rate in those days and people everywhere were accustomed to funerals with flag draped coffins and honor guards from the local VFW, but these were honest to goodness U.S. Air Force airmen. The closest airbase was over three hundred miles. And the Scotsman? Where did he come from and why?

The service began with the questions unanswered. As the minister looked up from his delivery of the last prayer, the otherwise quiet service was concluded with a twenty-one gun salute followed by a distant bugle playing Taps as the honor guard removed the flag from Jack's coffin, folded it properly and solemnly, and presented the folded flag to his grieving widow.

As Taps slowly echoed away across the rolling hills, a soulful rendition of Amazing Grace was played by the distant bagpiper, bringing tears to the eyes of all present, and the service to a somber end.

The silent and stunned crowd watched as the honor guard and the piper retreated to their vans without speaking, and slowly drove away. Several present pressed the funeral director and the minister with questions, and both men answered that they knew the honor guard was coming, but they didn't know why.

Many questions were never answered.

After the crowd dispersed, a lone man who had stood unnoticed as he watched the service from a nearby knoll walked slowly toward the grave. He was over six feet tall even though a damaged and arthritic spine had robbed him of over two inches in height. The deep seams and wrinkles on his face made evident the fact that he was very old, but he walked erect and projected the aura of one who was a leader. The man walked with the aid of a cane held in his right hand, but he didn't stoop or limp, and did not expose to the casual observer any indication of infirmity. On reaching the gravesite, he stood silently for several minutes while staring at the coffin.

Cemetery attendants were waiting to lower the coffin into the open grave, but they held back in deference to the old man who stood so erect, looking straight ahead. Finally, the man reached into the breast pocket of his jacket and retrieved a dark leather envelope. The small couriers' pouch was of a type commonly used during World War II. It was constructed of thick leather and lined on the inside with oilcloth. When closed and cinched tight with the leather straps, the package was waterproof and virtually indestructible by natural elements. Similar pouches were still occasionally unearthed across

Europe by farmers clearing land or tilling their fields, or at urban demolition or construction sites. Quite often, the contents of these packages were found to be intact and legible orders to field officers or intelligence about enemy troop movements, more than sixty years after being lost or discarded during World War II. After unwinding the leather cord that held the package closed, the old man removed its contents, a white linen envelope with no writing on the outside. He stared at it momentarily, the slightest hint of a smile on his lips, before replacing it into the leather pouch and tying the cord tightly around the package.

After a moment of reflection, he reached out to place the package on top of the coffin. "Jack, my old friend," he said quietly, "it is my greatest honor to finally deliver this to you. It should have happened long ago." He then stepped back one step, came to attention, and offered a crisp military salute to his fallen comrade. He was the only mourner in attendance who knew why the American and British honor guard had been present. He may have been the only one left in the world who knew the entire story. It was probably for the best. Who would believe that this kind, quiet old man from this little country town, whose life had been devoted to his family, church, and community for the last sixty years, a former private who only served six months of active military duty in 1943, did more than any other person in the world to defeat the Axis powers in WWII?

Chapter 2

May, 1943

Crack! The sharp noise and the solid feeling through the handle of the wooden bat told Jack he had made perfect contact. A brief glance revealed the baseball rocketing over the second baseman's glove as it threaded the space between the center and right fielders and headed to the outfield wall. Jack was a short man, but his churning legs had plenty of speed to bring him into second base with a stand-up double. He smiled and gave a thumbs up sign to the third base coach. Charlie Bradley had been his best friend since they had both dropped out of 9th grade to find needed work to help support their families during the depression years. Charlie had an uncanny ability to either steal signs from the catcher or to just *know* what the pitcher was about to throw. He had given Jack the sign to watch for a fast ball low and outside, and the pitch was delivered as promised, allowing Jack to give it a ride to right center field.

This was his third hit of the day. It was especially important to Jack that he played well, for this would be his last game as a Campbell Chick for a long time. He and Charlie had enlisted in the Army, along with thousands of other patriotic country boys across the nation, and would catch the bus for Fort Leonard Wood tomorrow to begin basic training. It was 1943 and America was at war.

An hour later the game was over. The Chicks had won their third in a row, this one five runs to four, and their season was off to a good start. The loss of Jack and Charlie was a severe one, but they had been training their own replacements, a couple of lanky, eighteen-year-old farm boys from over in the Four Mile Hill community. Lester, the taller one, could throw the ball faster than anyone on the team had ever seen. He could be a great pitcher, if only someone could teach him how to control the bullets that left his fingers. Right now Lester was as likely to kill the batters he faced as he was to strike them out, but maybe he could learn control...maybe.

Jack and Charlie received what seemed like hundreds of handshakes, pats on the back, and friendly punches in all four arms. They received requisite advice from fans and teammates...keep your head down, don't volunteer for anything, Jack you stay behind Charlie, Charlie you stay behind Jack, and so on. An old man in a wheel chair who was missing an arm and half a leg from WWI stopped them as they made their way through the small crowd. He grabbed Jack with his remaining arm and pulled him down close.

"I'm sorry, boy," he said, tears shimmering in his eyes. "My bunch didn't get the job done over there in 1918. Now you boys are havin' to go back and clean up after us." He nodded to the crowd around them and continued, "You do what these people said. You be careful and keep your head down. You be safe! But you also have to fight! You have to finish what we couldn't." He let go of Jack's arm and looked back and forth into the eyes of both men, rivulets of tears winding their way through the wrinkles in his cheeks. "War is a terrible, terrible thing," he said. "I'll pray for you every day, and the missus will, too. We'll pray you come home safe, and we'll pray you make this the very last war boys have to go and die in." He nodded, as if to indicate he was done, and continued to look at the ground until Jack and Charlie stepped away.

"Did you know that old guy?" Charlie asked after they had moved away from the crowd.

"Yeah," answered Jack." He lives a couple houses down the street from us. He was crippled up like that fightin' in the trenches in World War I in France, I think. Folks in the neighborhood say he was gassed with mustard gas, too. He can't walk very good, even when he has his fake leg, so he's usually in a wheel chair when I see him. That mustard gas does something bad to your nerves, they say. It cripples you for life. It's worse than a bullet."

Charlie wrinkled his brow, worried. "You think they still use that mustard gas over there?" he asked.

"I don't know," Jack answered quietly. "I don't even know who to ask. Maybe someone will know when we get to Fort Leonard Wood tomorrow night." He stopped walking and looked thoughtful for a moment before his face erupted into a huge grin. "What are we worried about, Charlie?" He slapped his friend hard on the back and continued, "That mustard gas can't be *half* as bad as that noxious stuff you fart out after about three days of a steady bean diet! *That* gas peels paint off the walls and makes your nerves stop working completely!" Jack smiled broadly. "I'll bet you a week's pay that we are completely immune to whatever mustard gas is."

The two young men walked in silence for several more blocks. Townspeople always called them Mutt and Jeff when they were seen together. Jack was short and solidly built, with muscular arms and a broad chest, strengthened by throwing watermelons, bales of hay, shovelfuls of coal, and anything else that might need to be moved by hand in the country community. Charlie was skinny and tall, already six feet but still growing so fast that his trousers always terminated a few inches shy of his ankles. He, too, worked the farms and anything else he could find, and was deceptively strong from the effort. The two men were quite different in many ways, but they were closer than many brothers; neither would have considered joining the Army to fight in places they had never heard of without the approval of the other.

When they reached the corner of First Street and Elm, Charlie turned left, looked over his shoulder, and said, "'Night, Jack. I'll see you at the bus stop first thing in the morning." He hung his head for a brief moment before saying, "I hope we're doing the right thing," and turned to walk on. Jack dreaded the tearful good-byes he knew would be waiting from his mom, baby brother, and two sisters. He knew his dad would accept his leaving stoically, but would feel the pain nonetheless.

With no one to hear his utterance, Jack whispered, "Yeah, Charlie. I hope we're doing the right thing, too." He looked up into the clear sky and stared momentarily at the full moon that was lighting his way. "I wonder if the moon looks the same over there where we're going?" The young man had many other questions, too. His life so far, as well as that of Charlie, had been lived within a small circle, both geographically and culturally. The bootheel on the southeastern side of Missouri had been his home his entire life and he rarely left it. Travel to nearby small towns was sometimes required to pick up supplies or equipment that was not locally available, but that kind of travel was within a comfortable sphere of recognizable farmland, cotton gins, and country stores. It didn't really qualify as "going somewhere."

Jack and Charlie had twice traveled by train to Memphis, which was one hundred forty miles away. On both occasions the two young men had hidden inside an empty railroad boxcar for the journey to and from their home, as neither of them could afford the price of a ticket. Hoboing, as it was known, was quite common, and they knew the likelihood of any punishment was very slight even if they were caught by the railroad police who occasionally inspected the open cars. The first trip to the city was eye-opening for the two boys, who made the first adventurous trip at age twelve. It was their first trip alone to such a large city, and even though they had no specific plans and only twelve cents between them, the pair wandered the downtown streets and the riverfront for hours.

The crowds of people, the city automobile traffic, and particularly the riverboats, captivated them. They had not made it back to the train yard until well after dark, and had waited for hours, tired and hungry, but too excited to complain, waiting for a train headed north to take them home. Their second trip to Memphis several years later was even more exciting. They had heard of something called the Mid-South Fair that was said to be the largest and most exciting carnival south of Chicago. Both men were seventeen at the time, and had dropped out of school a couple of years before to help support their families during the depression years. They planned for a year and saved a few cents from every payday for the trip. By the time opening day arrived, the two had saved over ten dollars each, a veritable fortune for the time. They still took public transport; that being the empty boxcar, to save the cost of transportation to Memphis, and thoroughly enjoyed themselves at the massive fair. The two arrived at about four p.m., paid the steep thirty five cents admission price (they could have gone to a movie for a nickel), and stayed until the midway closed at two a.m. and the carnies literally forced them to leave so the grounds could be cleaned up and readied for tomorrow's crowd.

Other trips were made more frequently to St. Louis, which was almost two hundred miles distant, but held more interest for Jack, Charlie, and others. St. Louis was home to Sportsman's Park and the St. Louis Cardinals baseball team. Every boy who grew up within a two hundred mile radius of the Gateway City, where Louis and Clark had launched their exploration of the western territories, listened to the Cardinal games whenever they could get near a radio. Every one of them dreamed of the day he could don a Cardinals uniform and race out onto the field with Dizzy Dean, Johnny Mize, and their newest hero in 1941, Stan Musial. At age seventeen, both Jack and Charlie were able to join the Campbell Chicks, one of the many semi-professional teams that traveled regionally and brought great baseball and entertainment to small communities throughout the nation. Whenever there was time, between the team's game schedule and the work schedules of the individual players, the entire team would load into the back of two or three farm trucks, often in uniform, and make the five-hour trip to Sportsman's Park to watch their heroes in action. Gasoline was rationed and expensive, almost twenty cents per gallon, but divided among twelve to fifteen players, fuel availability and cost of the trip was usually not prohibitive.

Jack thought of St. Louis and Memphis as he trudged home alone. Those cities represented the extent of his personal knowledge of the world. He had heard stories of other places, of course, but that was all he knew. He also had no knowledge of war, and what little he had heard from others didn't make it sound very enticing. The posters around town, however, said America needed men to join the Army and Navy. Many of Jack's friends as well as his older brother had enlisted and gone to war. It was his time, and he would not shirk his duty. Charlie wouldn't either. The two of them would make this trip with some excitement and a great deal of trepidation, but they would board that bus tomorrow with heads held high. Basic Training was to be at Fort Leonard Wood, Missouri, which was not too far away, so maybe the Army was planning to ease them into this drastic change of venue before hurling them into a fight half way around the world. Maybe it wouldn't be too bad, he thought to himself. Maybe the moon is just the same over there as it is here. The young man silently shook his head and walked home.

Chapter 3

Although their decision to enlist and go to war had been a mutual one, Jack and Charlie each had their own personal reasons for wanting to leave Campbell, Missouri for a life in the Army. Charlie was seeking excitement. He knew Campbell to be a safe and comfortable town, but a dull one in which nothing interesting ever happened. The only really exciting situation Charlie could remember had happened in late 1932, when he was only nine-years-old.

Charlie had been playing in the city park. An early snow had fallen on Thanksgiving Day, and he had left his house as soon as possible after the holiday meal. Being the only child in a room full of adults talking happily about adult things, Charlie knew he could find more interesting ways to spend his day off from school. Alone in the park, he gathered sticks and tree branches and began constructing a fort and small shelter between two trees. His structure was at the very back of the park in an area where park quickly turned into undeveloped woods, and was well hidden, even from the dirt road that passed by only a few yards away.

After examining his creation from all outside angles, Charlie crawled into his shelter, and was surprised to find it quite comfortable. There was no wind, and his own body heat seemed to warm the tiny enclosure very quickly. Bundled in his coat and mittens, his belly full of the wonderful Thanksgiving feast, the boy contentedly peered out the small window he had left facing the road for a few minutes until he became drowsy and fell asleep. He must have slept a few hours, for when he awoke it was late afternoon. It was still light, but the canopy of trees darkened this part of the park to a point that Charlie could see, but not clearly. A car had stopped on the road directly in front of his shelter. He almost screamed when the door opened and a large man stepped out holding a Tommy gun. Charlie clamped a gloved hand over his mouth and hoped he had not made any noise. He continued to stare wide-eyed out of his small window and soon relaxed as he realized the man, along with others who had joined him from the car, had not noticed him.

"Where is the old drunk?" the man with the machine gun bellowed. "He was supposed to meet us right here!"

"Hold it down, Manny," another voice said softly. "Voices travel a long way in this cold air and the police station is just a couple blocks away." After a short pause the same voice said, "Look, Manny, here comes someone now. It's probably old Virgil."

Hearing a muted cough in the distance, Manny pointed his Tommy gun in the direction of a shadowy figure shuffling slowly up the road toward the car. Charlie was shocked once more when the three other men in the group produced pistols from their pockets and aimed them at the figure. The boy knew old Virgil

Anderson, who was known to be a bootlegger and the town drunk, and hoped this bunch wasn't about to kill him.

As Virgil approached and saw the weapons pointed at him, he raised his hands over his head and said in a gravelly voice, "Sorry boys. City only has one police car, and it just happened to be patrolling along my street as I was leaving. I had to take back roads to get here."

"Git in the car!" Manny growled as he grabbed old Virgil by the shoulder and shoved him into the back seat. Three of the men put their pistols back into their pockets and climbed into the car. The one called Manny stayed outside for a few minutes and slowly looked around, moving the muzzle of the Thompson submachine gun in the direction he was looking. For a brief moment, the terrible weapon was pointed directly at Charlie, but the boy willed himself to stay frozen in position, making no sound. In a moment, the danger passed as Manny handed the gun to someone in the car, then slid behind the steering wheel and closed the door. He started the engine and slowly drove away.

Charlie had not realized he was holding his breath, but finally released it, watching for a moment the fog it formed while mingling with the cold evening air. He crawled from his shelter and ran all the way home to tell his parents what he had seen.

It was three days before Charlie finally heard the entire story. One of his older friends, a boy in the tenth grade, was the son of a state patrolman. He learned the details of the incident from his father and passed it on to a spellbound group of boys in the school cafeteria. John Dillinger was a notorious bank robber who ranged throughout the Midwest during the depression years. The FBI had been chasing him, and during November of 1932 agents were closing in on Dillinger and several of his gang at a hideout in Springfield, Illinois. The wily bank robber divided his gang into three groups and sent them in different directions, hopefully confusing the feds. Dillinger himself fled north to Chicago, where he remained hidden for over a year before being killed by FBI agents led by Melvin Purvis.

More important to Charlie and the citizens of southeast Missouri, four of the Dillinger gang fled south from Springfield with a goal of reaching Hattiesburg, Mississippi. Fearing that agents were on their trail in Illinois, the group crossed into Missouri via the Grafton Ferry and proceeded south toward the bootheel. Short of money, the four men decided on impulse to rob the bank in the small town of Poplar Bluff. Three armed men robbed the teller windows on the day before Thanksgiving while the fourth man waited in the car at the front door. Their total take was six hundred and seventeen dollars, not a great haul, but not too bad for poverty stricken farm country in the midst of the Great Depression.

The four men drove southeast from Poplar Bluff on U.S. Highway 53 and spent the night in a barn outside of Qulin, Missouri. Roads were slick on Thanksgiving morning, so they stayed in the barn until early afternoon, hoping the snow and ice would melt enough for them to drive. Finally leaving the barn, they continued on Highway 53 for a few miles before crossing the St. Francis River on the only bridge available in the county. Fearful of police patrolling the highway, they turned onto a gravel road that wound through the countryside toward Campbell, Missouri. Benny Oxley, son of a Qulin bootlegger, had brought the men dinner while they were in the barn, a simple meal of hot biscuits and butter the young man had stolen from his mother's kitchen. The bank robbers asked Benny for directions to Kennett, Missouri via back roads to avoid the highways. The young man didn't know, but said he knew someone who could guide them there. "Give me an hour," he told the bank robbers, "and meet a man named Virgil on the dirt road behind the city park in Campbell. He may be drunk, he usually is, but he can get you safe to Kennett."

After picking up Virgil and scaring Charlie out of a year's growth, the gang headed south out of Campbell on a dirt road that paralleled Highway 53 to Holcomb. Unknown to the men, federal agents had warned the Missouri State Police that part of the Dillinger gang was headed south, and would probably keep to the back roads in an effort to avoid detection. The Dunklin County Sheriff and the State Police had cars patrolling all likely country roads, and only a few miles south of Campbell found the old sedan speeding along. Two police cars with lights flashing and sirens blaring chased the car for five miles before Manny slammed on the brakes, causing the sedan to slip on the ice and plow into a shallow roadside ditch. Doors flew open and the robbers emerged guns in hand and began shooting at the police, who quickly returned fire.

Five minutes later the shootout was over. One county deputy sheriff lay on the icy road wounded, but he would live. Two of the gang members had been killed and one sat shakily in the front seat of the sedan moaning and holding a gash that started at the corner of his left eye and traveled around his skull to the back. He was also missing the upper third of his left ear. Of the four gang members, only Manny had emerged unscathed and stood beside the sedan with his hands raised. Virgil had not been hurt, and, unknown to the police, had been cowering in the back seat of the sedan the entire time. He surprised the officers by jumping from the car and immediately reaching into the inside breast pocket of his old and frayed coat. His intent was to grab a bottle of bootleg whiskey from the pocket and throw the contraband into the ditch before he could be arrested for it. The police naturally thought he was reaching for a gun, and three of them fired at the old man, killing Virgil instantly.

Charlie's friend who was relating the story to his spellbound audience slowly shook his head and cast his eyes downward. He finished the tale by saying, "Daddy says that whiskey will kill you every time!"

It was an exciting few days, Charlie had to admit, but looking back on his twenty years in Campbell, it was the only real excitement he could remember. He wanted more.

**

Jack's reasons for joining the Army and going to war were more basic, more personal. Like Charlie, he yearned for a more exciting life and dreamed of the romantic notion of traveling abroad and fighting for freedom. Closer to home for Jack, however, was the story Jack's older brother, Bill, had told him while on a recent leave from the Navy. The story was actually classified at the time and Bill could have been court marshaled for telling the tale, but the men were brothers, after all, and Bill felt the need to tell the tragic story to someone, regardless of orders.

Times were tough in rural Missouri, and as much from a desire to have a steady job as from a sense of patriotism, Bill had joined the U.S. Navy soon after the war had begun. In mid 1942 he had been assigned to the light cruiser USS Juneau. His shipboard duties were to act as barber for the crew of almost seven hundred and, in case of attack, back-up gunner on the #4 deck gun. During a night battle with a Japanese task force near Guadalcanal on November 13, 1942, the Juneau was struck on the port side by a torpedo, and was disabled to such a degree that it had to withdraw from the battle. The night action was fought at practically point blank range, and heavy losses were incurred on both sides. Limping away from the battle within a group of other damaged American ships, the Juneau was struck a second time by a Japanese torpedo in almost exactly the same spot as the first hit. This second torpedo ignited a midships powder magazine and literally blew the ship in half. A majority of the crew was killed in the attack, but approximately one hundred fifteen men were able to jump into the water before the ship sank.

Other ships in the convoy were unable to stop to pick up survivors, but radioed in the coordinates so the Navy could send other ships or aircraft to pick them up when the area was safe. During the chaos of battle, however, the message was never received. The surviving crew of the Juneau floated in the water for eight days before anyone was sent to search for them. Wounds, hypothermia, and shark attacks slowly whittled down the helpless crew until a rescue vessel finally arrived. Only ten crewmen remained. Jack's brother Bill was one of the lucky ten.

The incident was tragic on several levels, but one tragedy that caused great consternation to the Navy and the War Department was the loss of the Sullivan family; five brothers who were serving together on the USS Juneau. Navy policy of the time was not to allow brothers to serve together, but the brothers had specifically requested assignment together, and in this case the Navy overlooked its own regulation. Due to the chaotic circumstances, reports were never completely verified, but it was believed that two of the brothers were killed during the explosion and sinking of the cruiser. The other three escaped into the water, but were lost during the eight day wait before the few survivors were rescued.

For many reasons—the loss of several ships and over a thousand men during the battle, the fact that the Navy had failed to follow its own policy, and the tragic loss of the entire Sullivan family, the Navy clamped down on any news of the battle or the loss of life. In normal circumstances, survivors of a ship sunk during a battle were given an immediate thirty day survivors' leave. In the case of the USS Juneau, however, leave was not granted for the few survivors for over four months. When the leave was finally granted, it came with strict orders not to discuss the battle, the sinking of the Juneau, or the Sullivan brothers with anyone.

When Bill finally came home in May of 1943, it was to a family that had been worried. He had not written and there had been no news of his whereabouts for over six months. When pressed by his family for the reason he had not written them, he said only that he had been in the South Pacific and with so many battles going on in the area there was not time for mail service. It was only to Jack that he told the entire story, swearing his younger brother to secrecy lest Bill spend the rest of his life in military prison.

After hearing the story, Jack decided it was time for him to leave the safety of Campbell and civilian life. It was time to go to war.

Chapter 4

Army Basic Training wasn't bad at all, at least as far as Jack and Charlie could see. They were mustered in together, and by the luck of the draw were assigned to the same platoon for the six week training course. They even bunked together, Jack on the top bunk of the stacked pair, and Charlie on the bottom.

The first few days were almost like a vacation, something neither of the friends had ever experienced. The days were filled with test taking, filling out paperwork, standing in long lines to be given uniforms, socks, helmets, and, at last, their own rifles, M-14s ready for combat! They were taught to stand at attention, march, salute, and many other things that were foreign and new to them, but were probably important for military life. Most important, they were provided with three square meals every day. Even though some of the city boys complained about the food (actually, they complained about everything), Jack and Charlie thought it was about the best food they had ever tasted. Sometimes there were even seconds and dessert.

"Charlie," Jack said as they moved through the chow line on their third day of basic, "you know what you said to me that last night we were home? You hoped we were doing the right thing?" Charlie nodded, and Jack held up his tray heaping with fried chicken, dumplings, green beans, and apple sauce. "I think we did good," he said.

Charlie grinned and nodded his agreement.

"You guys stop talking in the chow line!" the drill sergeant bellowed. Jack and Charlie just nodded and grinned.

Both young men had grown up in farm country, and from the time they could tie their own shoes, had worked on farms and whatever other odd jobs they could find around town to earn a dollar and help provide for their families. Charlie was an only child and, as such, had only himself and his parents to provide for. By the time he was ten-years-old, Jack was the third of eight siblings, two of which had died in a whooping cough epidemic in 1929. It was a large family to feed through the depression years, but all the boys and their dad found work wherever it was to be had, and the family did okay. Even the two baby sisters, aged four and seven, turned out in the fall to pick cotton and make a few pennies.

Jack and Charlie both knew hard work, and had grown strong walking or running, often for several miles to jobs...pitching hundred pound bales of hay into barn lofts, chopping or picking cotton in ninety degree heat, or unloading tons of coal from railroad freight cars. Compared to their civilian lives, Army life was pretty easy, and they fell into the routine with little trouble. The city boys, many of whom were from St.

Louis and Kansas City, although some were from far away exotic places like New Orleans and New York City, complained. They complained about the miles of running, the early reveille, the push-ups, and just about all else related to their training. Jack and Charlie just shook their heads in amazement and tried to fit in. They were certain it would sound crazy to most of their fellow trainees, but they were having fun.

At the end of basic, both men and the rest of their platoon marched proudly at the graduation ceremony to the tunes of John Phillip Sousa played by a real brass band. They were strong, ramrod straight, and pleased to be soldiers. They thought they were ready for anything the enemy could throw their way.

The battery of tests given throughout the weeks of basic training had revealed that Charlie possessed strong organizational skills. He was assigned after basic to a school that would teach him to be a military administrative specialist. He reported the assignment to Jack with an air of disgust. "What is an, uh, administrative specialist?" Charlie asked.

"I'm not sure," Jack answered cautiously. "Didn't they tell you?"

"Nah, nobody said anything. It sounds like some kind of glorified company clerk...you know, the geeky guy who hands out our weekend passes and sits in front of that typewriter all day at HQ."

Jack considered for a minute before answering, "Might not be so bad. I notice our company clerk doesn't get shot at very often."

"Where are you headed, Jack?" Charlie asked, nodding at the orders his friend held in his hand.

Jack held out the paper and answered, "Army Air Corps gunnery school. I guess all those years of shooting squirrels and rabbits paid off." He smiled. "I'll bet I could *really* bring home dinner with a fifty caliber machine gun."

Charlie looked at the orders with jealous eyes. "Wow! I sure wish..."

He was unable to finish the thought because another private, who they had noticed jogging across the compound, stopped when he reached them. Glancing at the name tag sewn on Jack's uniform, he said without inflection, "You're wanted at the base commander's office, ASAP."

Both men stared at the messenger for a few seconds, until Jack began to laugh.

You're kidding, right? Did Jamison put you up to this?"

The messenger only looked grim.

Jack pressed, "You're talking about *the* base commander, Brigadier General Armstrong? You know, I've never even seen an officer higher than a captain from less than a hundred yards away." He glanced at Charlie. "I'm not even sure colonels and generals are *real*...maybe just a made up rank to stand somewhere between us enlisted men and *God!"*

The messenger was unfazed. "The general is waiting. I suggest you get moving."

Fifteen minutes later, Jack was standing nervously at attention in front of a desk just outside a door that announced 'Brigadier General J. T. Armstrong.' "Relax, private," said the master sergeant sitting at the desk, a soldier with so many stripes on his sleeve and ribbons on his chest that he was possibly more intimidating to Jack than the prospect of standing before an honest-to-God general. The master sergeant continued in a calming tone, "I'll tell you, I've seen the general rip into a few majors and colonels and make 'em wish they was standing in front of a firing squad instead of him." Jack tried to swallow, but found his throat was too dry. The sergeant went on, "But I have never seen him so much as holler at a private...he respects you guys...he knows whenever he barks an order, it is ultimately the privates who do the work and fightin' he wants done. It'll be all right, Private. Relax."

The sergeant's phone rang. He picked up the receiver, listened for a few moments, then replied, "Yes, sir, I will take care of that." After another moment of silence, he said, "Yes, sir, I'll send in the private now." After hanging up the receiver, he nodded to Jack and, indicating the general's door with a lean of his head, said, "Knock three times, then enter immediately. Don't speak until you are spoken to." With just a hint of a knowing smile, he continued, "It'll be okay, Private. You have the word of an old enlisted man."

Moments later the young private was standing silently at rigid attention in front of the base commander's desk. Rivulets of nervous sweat were streaming down his forehead and into his eyes, making them sting, but he was not about to move in any way to relieve the pain. General Armstrong looked up from his paperwork and into Jack's eyes. "At ease, son." he said in a surprisingly soft and kind voice. With what looked like amusement on his face, he opened a desk drawer, retrieved a paper tissue from a small pack, and held it across the desk to the nervous soldier. "Here, wipe the sweat out of your eyes. You need to be able to see me clearly while we talk."

Jack tentatively reached out to retrieve the tissue. He wasn't certain at this point whether he should smile, salute, run, or just melt into the plank floor, but he mumbled a quiet, "Thank you, sir," and looked quizzically at the tissue, having never seen one before. The general made a motion of dabbing his forehead and eyes, and Jack followed the example, feeling immediate relief from the stinging sweat as he wiped it from his eyes. "Thank you, sir," he said more firmly as his vision cleared and the pain subsided.

General Armstrong glanced down at a file on his desk, allowing a few moments for Jack to glance around the small office. A row of three opened windows directly behind the general's chair provided the only air circulation into the small room. One wall was covered with photographs, most of which were of Armstrong in various stages of his military career posing with fellow officers. In the center was a photo of a very young Captain Armstrong shaking hands with a four-star general who appeared to be John J. Pershing. Jack was so mesmerized by the photograph that he failed to notice when General Armstrong looked up at him. The private started and jerked back to attention when the general arose from his chair and stepped toward the wall of photos.

"General Blackjack Pershing," he said in a reverent tone. "Possibly the most famous soldier in the history of the modern Army. I was privileged to serve under him several years ago...back when I had hair," he said with a chuckle, rubbing a hand across his mostly bald pate. Armstrong took the photo from the wall, stared at it for a brief moment, then moved around his desk and handed it to Jack, who found himself becoming more nervous as the general approached. He indicated a small table with two chairs in one corner of the room. "Have a seat, son...we need to talk."

Jack looked at him with questions in his eyes. Sitting in the presence of a general was surely not proper military etiquette. Was the general trying to trick him into doing something wrong? That didn't seem right, either. "Sir?" was the only question he could make himself utter.

"It's all right," Armstrong offered with a smile. "You sit there," he indicated a chair, "and I'll take the other chair."

Jack sat on the front edge of the wooden chair, his back still ramrod straight as if he was still at attention. The general sat opposite him, reached across the table, and took the photo from the private's hands. "Do you know anything about General Pershing?" he asked.

"I know who he is...or, maybe, was," Jack answered. "I recognized him in the picture, and I know he was a great general in World War I, but that's about all, I guess." He paused for a moment before adding with emphasis, "Sir!"

The general smiled and looked with admiration at the photo. "Ole Blackjack is still alive and kicking...lives in Washington, D.C. so he can still be close to the action, so to speak." He looked up from the photo and into Jack's eyes. "Do you know, he was just a little boy, of course, but he remembers the fighting around his house in Laclede, Missouri during the Civil War? I find that amazing. A living American General who can remember the Civil War." Armstrong pierced the young private with his stare for a long minute, finally saying, "General Pershing is part of the reason I wanted to see you today. Your service record during basic training is the rest of the reason."

Jack was silent, trying to conceal his confusion and complete lack of understanding. He shifted in his chair, but said nothing. Finally, the commanding officer began. "General Pershing was commander of the American Expeditionary Force in World War I. Europe was in bad trouble, and the force was assembled quickly in 1917. But the general made a mistake...he insisted that every member of the Force be trained to the highest possible degree. That sounds like a good idea, but he took almost an entire year to get the Expeditionary Force trained to the point he was satisfied they were ready. Europe suffered greatly during that year of training. The German Army had time to entrench itself...build fortifications and strengthen lines so when the American force finally reached Europe, the job was much more difficult than it might have been if Blackjack had acted quickly." He stopped for a moment before asking, "Do you understand?"

For a moment, Jack just nodded. Suddenly realizing his egregious breach of military protocol, he stiffened and answered in a shaky voice, "Oh, sorry, Sir. Yes, Sir, I think I understand. Our allies were in trouble and General Pershing could have helped them more if he had gotten there a little quicker. It's better not to let the enemy dig in if we can stop them."

"Right. Good." Armstrong said brightly. "Your company commander was right. You catch on quickly. Now, moving from World War I up to today, we have a situation in Europe similar to that of 1917. Much of the continent is in Hitler's grip, and his grip is tightening. This information is highly classified, so I can't tell you much, but we are planning something big...bigger than the American Expeditionary Force...to take Europe back. I may be a general, but I'm a very small cog in a very large machine that is putting together a massive force as quickly as possible to free our allies from the Nazis."

He paused for a moment, his eyes narrowing. "Unlike Pershing, we will not wait a year before deploying the force. We will do it almost as quickly as we can assemble the men, and we will train them in rapid stages as we move toward the front lines. Because of that schedule—something that has never been tried—we need to assemble a very select force composed of men who can learn quickly, who can withstand adversity without complaint, and who can think on the run and handle just about anything that is thrown their way." He picked up Jack's thin service record, comprised only of reports and test results from his few weeks in basic training, and glanced at it briefly.

Jack glanced at the file and back up to General Armstrong. "Sir, are you sure that messenger meant to get *me?* I'm just a private, and I don't know much about..."

"You're the man." The general interrupted. He tapped on the brown file cover. "This says you learn quickly, you can plan and build small fortifications, you follow orders without question or complaint, you can shoot, you can solve problems as an individual and as a team member, you can both lead men and follow leadership. This says you can handle just about any task we order you to do." He removed his hand from the file and stared intently at the young man. "One thing you probably don't know is how incredibly rare it is to find all those abilities and attributes in one young recruit. The Army doesn't see that often, son, but we always recognize it and always find the best possible ways to use soldiers like you."

Armstrong pushed his chair back and stood, a movement that made Jack reflexively jerk to attention, in the process knocking his chair over, and bumping the table forward into the general's thighs. The officer only smiled as he moved toward his desk. "At ease, Private...at ease." He opened a drawer and retrieved a single sheet of paper. "You have orders to report to gunnery school," he stated.

Jack nodded, and then caught himself. "Yes, sir," he said firmly.

Armstrong handed him the paper. "Those orders are countermanded. You are to report to a newly formed unit, the 925th Engineer Aviation Regiment. This outfit will be made up of officers and men just like you, who can train quickly, move quickly, and get the job done quickly and efficiently." His stare intensified. "It's an honor, son. It means your soldiering skills are top shelf. Hell, I'm kind of jealous. I wasn't picked for this new unit...you and four other boys from my command were picked, along with hundreds of others just like you from all around the world."

Jack was confused, and finally mustered the courage to ask the general a question. "Sir, why are you telling me this...I mean you, personally? Why didn't I just get new orders?"

"Because it's top secret, Private." Armstrong barked. "Nobody knows about this new unit except you, me, and the other men being assigned to the 925th. No one else in this command knows, and no one *will know*. The plans are such that the 925th will be in a theater of operations long before the enemy even knows the unit exists. I'm only telling you this much because you will not be able to tell anyone else. You leave today."

Jack had been at rigid attention ever since the general had raised his voice, but tried to stiffen even more so. "Yes sir!" he said crisply. "I'll just go to the barracks and..."

"No." Armstrong interrupted. More softly he said, "I'm sorry, son, but you won't even have time to say good-bye to your friends. There's a jeep just outside waiting to take you to the airfield. The driver has already picked up your duffel. A C-47 transport is waiting to fly you and the others to March Field in California, where you will begin a very brief and intense training assignment until shipping out."

The general sat down at his desk. "That's all, Private. Good luck."

Chapter 5

Four and a half hours later Jack was sitting in a canvas strap seat bolted to the frame of a C-47 cargo plane. The aircraft had been flying directly into a stiff headwind since takeoff, making forward progress much slower than the one hundred sixty mph cruise speed of the workhorse craft. Three other enlisted men and one officer, a rather sour looking captain, were belted into similar seats in the belly of the airplane. They didn't speak. The incessant noise and vibration from the twin 1350 horsepower Curtis-Wright radial engines passed through the thin, uninsulated metal of the fuselage as if it was no barrier at all, making any attempt at conversation futile. The Douglas DC-3 aircraft, designated C-47 by the Army Air Corps, was never designed for comfort. During World War II, the workhorse craft carried supplies, machinery, and men virtually all over the world. Its hold could be loaded with a fully assembled Jeep or a thirty-seven millimeter cannon. It could carry a small platoon of men in full gear ready for combat or more than a dozen wounded on stretchers, along with doctors and nurses to care for them. The aircraft was designed for utility, not comfort, a fact that had become very clear to the California bound passengers on this flight. The five men tried to sleep, but the constant dips and jolts from air pockets and crosswinds made that endeavor impossible. The captain had thought to bring along a newspaper, which he attempted to read as it bumped and rattled in his hands. The four enlisted men just looked at each other or at the floor with tired eyes, wondering when this ordeal would end.

After a brief fuel stop at Fort Bliss, Texas, they took off once more with a heading for Southern California. As the aircraft climbed above the desert heat, it became apparent that this leg of the trip would be much smoother than earlier one, and with the headwind abated, the pilot was able to throttle back the engines to make the hold much quieter and more comfortable.

Four hours later, the co-pilot came out of the flight cabin to awaken the soldiers, who had finally been lulled to sleep by the steady drone of the engines. "Any of you guys ever seen an ocean?" He shouted over the engines.

All five shook their heads, prompting the Lieutenant to say, "March Field is about fifty miles inland from the Pacific, but the captain said he would make a wide swing to the west so you can see the vast blue if you're interested." All five nodded their heads in unison. Even the sour captain smiled and gave the Lieutenant a thumbs up sign.

Jack was so completely mesmerized by the ocean that he forgot anyone else was on the flight. After his first glance out the window, he unfastened his seat belt and stood gripping either side of the window with his nose pressed against the glass. The blue went on forever. He had seen the Mississippi River and several large lakes in his little sliver of the world, but never imagined anything like this. From a thousand feet, he could see a port below the aircraft that contained several large ships. Offshore were a few others, and the white triangles of two sailing vessels were visible in the distance. Beyond them was only water for as far as he could see. How far did it go? Jack remembered studying that at some time when he was in school, but didn't remember.

After their brief tour over Los Angeles and the ocean, the aircraft touched down at March Field. The passengers were surprised to be met at the aircraft door by a deuce-and-a-half ready to whisk them away from the air strip. "In here!" were the only words spoken by a staff sergeant as he indicated the back of the truck. The men and their equipment were quickly loaded, and the heavy canvas cover was lowered over the back, engulfing them in darkness just before the gears ground together and the truck lurched to a start.

Their ears were still ringing from the C-47, but the back of the truck was relatively quiet, prompting Jack to ask, "Captain? Sir, do you have any idea what's going on or where they're taking us?"

After a few seconds of silence, the officer answered, "Sorry, men. You probably know as much as I do, which is basically nothing. I can tell you this, though. Whatever it is we're doing, we're obviously about to do it really fast."

The captain was right...the next four weeks were a blur of training. MOS is the United States Army's acronym for Military Occupation Specialty. The Army traditionally has hundreds of MOS job descriptions, of which most soldiers are assigned only one. The 925th did not follow military convention in that respect, however, and put the troops through a rapid-fire instructional program designed in such a way that each soldier was taught to perform several tasks. The regiment was primarily an aviation engineering group, tasked to build runways, housing, camouflage and other details essential to flight operations. Since the force's primary task required moving rapidly to work with several different fighter and bomber groups, the soldiers were also taught the basics of crewing, loading ordinance, and flight operations of several different aircraft.

Jack quickly understood the reason the general back at Fort Leonard Wood had emphasized the need for trainees who could learn quickly and without complaint. There were days when so much was thrown at the men there was no time to eat anything other than an apple on the run, or a ham sandwich that could be wolfed down in three bites while carrying a tool box or a weapon in the other hand. It was a good group of men. There were few complaints about the unusually rigorous schedule, and the few gripes that were aired were done more so as humor than real distress.

The only thing even remotely resembling a break in their rigid schedule came on the morning when

Lieutenant Horne ordered an entire company of men, Jack included, hurriedly loaded into trucks to travel fifty miles east of the base and help the undermanned United States Forest Service fight a large forest fire that was threatening homes in the San Jacinto Mountains. The fire raged for three days, but finally the soldiers were able to contain it to a point that the grateful Forest Service firefighters were able manage on their own.

Delta Company rushed back to March Field in trucks filled with dirty and exhausted men who were given only a couple of hours to clean the smoke smell out of their hair and clothes, then eat a quick meal before being thrown back into the rigors of the unrelenting training schedule.

By the time the course was completed, Jack was able to operate a transit level, grade a flat runway with a bulldozer, build a Quonset hut, lay a mile of metal tracking for flight operations in wet or marshy areas, construct a floating bridge, and a variety of other engineering tasks. It was a great deal for only twenty-seven days of training, but along with it, he had taken classes and received some practical experience in air traffic control, loading ordinance onto B-17 and B-26 bombers, and the basics of flight navigation.

By far his favorite part of the training blitz, however, was the two days he spent in aviation gunnery school, during which he was thrilled to fly in B-17s, B-25s, and even a brand new B-24 Liberator that had been flown straight from the San Diego factory to

March Field for crew training. While learning to fire fifty caliber machine guns from a variety of positions at targets strategically placed throughout the Southern California desert, Jack realized he had found his military calling. I finally made it to gunnery school, the young private thought with pride. He had just shredded a large paper target mounted on the peak of a low mountain as the B-17 raced by at nearly two hundred mph, and was looking though the window of the starboard waist gun at the destruction with a smile on his face. Hands on his shoulders pulled him away from the window. "Short bursts of ammo, airman...short bursts," said the flight engineer, a second lieutenant who served as turret gunner, engineer, aircraft repairman, and crew chief on these training missions. "You killed that target with your first two bullets. Don't waste ammunition!" He smiled and patted Jack roughly on his right shoulder. "Good job, soldier...good shooting!"

**

As Jack deplaned from his second training flight he looked across the tarmac and froze in his tracks. Not a hundred yards away sat a Lockheed P-38 Lightning, the most beautiful aircraft ever constructed, at least in the private's opinion. It was a twin engine, twin boom, single seat fighter and bomber known by the Germans as the "forked-tale devil" for its appearance and destructive capabilities. Jack had never seen one up close, and was not to be denied this opportunity. Since the fighter was a single seat craft with no gunnery position, Jack would never get to train in one.

He jogged the short distance to the Lightning and, finding no one around and the hatch open, brushed aside all thought of getting into trouble and decided to climb inside. Sitting in the pilot's seat with his hand on the control stick, Jack lost all track of time as he imagined himself blasting his way through an entire flight of Me-109s and watching them flee in terror before his deadly guns.

He awoke from his dream when a voice boomed, "Hey! What are you doing in there?" Jack scurried from the seat and out of the aircraft red faced, embarrassed, and fearful of reprimand. He came to attention in front of an angry looking lieutenant colonel. "What were you doing in my P-38?" the colonel demanded.

Jack stammered, "I'm sorry, sir." He indicated the B-17 parked in the distance. "I just finished a gunnery training flight and saw this...this beautiful airplane and had to take a look." He hung his head. "I got carried away, I guess, sir." He looked pleadingly into the officer's eyes. "Probably my only chance to actually touch a P-38, sir."

To the young man's surprise, the officer cast a sympathetic look as he held out a hand to touch the silver skin of the aircraft. "I get it, Private," he said softly. "I have almost a thousand hours flight time in this baby, and she's still as beautiful as the day I first saw her." He backed up a step and looked at Jack. "You took quite a chance."

"Yes, sir," Jack answered. "And again, I'm sorry sir. Guess I wanted to touch a P-38 more than I worried about any trouble I might get myself into."

The pilot chuckled as he reached into his pocket. "I'll tell you what, Private. I'll forget this incident ever happened if you will promise to stay away from any aircraft you are not authorized to be around. Deal?"

Jack quickly nodded. "Yes, sir. Deal."

The lieutenant colonel held out a small object he had retrieved from his pocket. "Take this, Private. The next time *you're* tempted to touch a P-38, find this in your pocket and touch it!"

Jack looked at the small piece of metal in his palm and began to laugh. It was a tiny can opener, developed by the Army as a compact way to open C-Ration food cans in the field. Only about an inch long and hinged with a small sharp blade, the opener was commonly known throughout the Army as a P-38 due to the fact that it required thirty-eight punctures to work its way around the top of the C-Ration can to open it.

"A P-38!" Jack said in amazement. He looked up at the officer, still laughing. "Thank you, sir. I'll remember that." He stopped laughing, but still had a broad grin on his face as he came to attention and saluted the officer.

The lieutenant colonel retuned the salute with a compassionate smile. "Good luck, soldier. Shoot straight."

Jack walked away staring at the can opener in his hand and laughing once more.

As the sun was sinking behind the hills just west of the field on July 31, 1943, bone weary troops of the 925th Engineer Aviation Regiment were boarding a train destined for their staging area, Camp Kilmer, New Jersey. Thirty days before, the 925th had existed only on paper. Now it was a group of highly trained, multitalented, albeit tired and bedraggled, American soldiers who were ready to do whatever was asked of them. Rumors and questions were rampant throughout the train. Is this it? Are we headed for war? Will it be Europe, Africa, or the Pacific? Answers to all of those questions abounded and spread quickly, but the fact was that only the Regimental Commander and a select few of his superiors in Washington, D.C. knew of the nature and mission of the 925th.

Soldiers jostled and squirmed into narrow seats as the Atchison, Topeka, and Santa Fe locomotive jerked the specially chartered train to a start, the massive steel wheels spinning fruitlessly for a few moments until finally gaining purchase on the tracks beneath them. The line of rail cars buzzed with anxious questions, nervous laughter, and excitement for the first few miles, then became quiet as the regiment, almost en mass, was lulled to sleep by the monotonous clack-clack of the rails below them. Their rigorous training had denied them of much needed rest for too long, and whether by design or sheer chance, the four-day train journey across the breadth of the United States would give them a much deserved respite. Due to the urgency and secrecy of the 925th's mission, the train made only brief, necessary stops, and no soldier was allowed to disembark.

On August 4 the train finally reached Camp Kilmer, New Jersey, a staging area chosen by the War Department for its proximity to New York City and its ports of embarkation for troops deploying to the European theater of operations. Every member of the 925th was anxious to escape the cramped confines of the train, breathe fresh air, and stretch their cramped muscles. Most platoons were put through a series of calisthenics immediately after disembarking the train but, surprisingly, no one complained, as the men welcomed the chance to exercise. The next few days were filled with inspections, crating of necessary equipment to be shipped overseas, more inspections, and even more inspections. Initial plans, known only to a few high ranking officers at Camp Kilmer and the Pentagon, were to ship out the entire regiment after only twelve days of preparation in the staging area. A minor snafu in transportation, however, prevented some vital equipment from reaching New Jersey in a timely manner, causing the entire deployment to be postponed for almost two weeks.

While generals fumed and several heads doubtlessly rolled because of the delay, on a more local level, company officers decided to issue twelve hour passes to most of the troops as a minor reward for their weeks of hard work. Private Adrian Burrow, a native of nearby New York City and a member of Jack's squad, offered to take his friends into the city for a tour of all the famous spots. After a lively discussion, the group decided they would rather go to a baseball game. The Brooklyn Dodgers were in town playing the St. Louis Cardinals, and none of the men could imagine a better way to spend at least part of their free time.

Both professional teams were depending on aging players because many of the younger stars were off to war. Despite the brush strokes of grey hair hidden under many of their baseball caps, both teams played well in the back and forth game. Cardinal pitcher Al Brazie went the distance, and recorded a seven-three win. The Dodgers hammered out eight hits, but only plated three runs. Brooklyn's starting pitcher, Ed Head, was relieved in the sixth inning by Les Webber, but was still recorded as the losing pitcher. One particularly entertaining moment, that brought a loud chorus of boos from the hometown crowd, occurred when Dodger manager Leo Durocher was thrown out of the game in the seventh after he charged out of the dugout and kicked dirt at the home plate umpire to express his disgust with a call that brought the inning to an end.

The mid-week crowd was sparse, and the soldiers were surprised when, early in the ninth inning, the announcer broadcast an invitation for anyone in military uniform to come down to the field after the game and meet the players. Jack and the entire group were able to shake hands and talk with many of their baseball idols, including Howie Schultz, Billy Herman, and Luis Olmo. By sheer happenstance, New York Yankee slugger Joe DiMaggio was in town for an Army Air Corps publicity tour. The Yanks were out of town, and Joe had come out to watch the game and greet some old friends. DiMaggio had joined the Army in February, just before spring training had started, and was in his Army Air Corps uniform. Jack and his friends were amazed to find that the Yankee Clipper was only a private, just like them! Private Joe was accompanied by veteran pitcher Bobo Newsome, who had become famous years before, not for his pitching, but for a statement he made to a sportswriter during DiMaggio's rookie season with the Yankees. The writer had asked Newsome if he knew anything about the lanky rookie outfielder. "Yeah," Newsome answered dryly, "he has a weakness for doubles."

Several of the Cardinals also came over to greet the soldiers. Jack was in sports heaven when he was able to shake hands and share a joke with Lou Klein, Whitey Kurowski, and Walker Cooper, players he had often seen on the field after traveling to St. Louis, but never dreamed of actually meeting in person. When the Cardinals' players discovered Jack was a big fan who lived not far from St. Louis, they made sure he was given a signed baseball and several Red Bird caps. Cards' slugging phenom Stan Musial actually took off his jersey, signed it across the back, and draped it across Jack's shoulders.

With a broad smile and bright eyes, he said, "You be safe, kid. Come to St. Louis when you get back home. Let me know and I'll have seats for you right behind the dugout."

Chapter 6

"Load up, you lugs!" was the shouted order at five p.m. on August 29. The 925th loaded equipment and men into another train and made the short journey to the Port of Embarkation in New York City. While no official word had been given, each of the men had a feeling in his gut that this was the big one...they were going off to war. Exactly where they were going, no one seemed to know. It was after dark when they reached the port, and near midnight before the entire regiment was loaded onto several ferries that moved slowly across the black water to their next destination.

After an hour on the water, the lights of a huge steam ship had grown to a point that the men could read the name printed in large letters on the bow of the craft...Queen Elizabeth. They were going to board the Queen Elizabeth, the stately Cunard liner pressed into service as a troop carrier, for their journey across the Atlantic. Jack trudged up the long gangway onto the famous ship just behind Private Burrow at two fifteen a.m. on August 30, 1943. The two men had become close friends, and both looked downcast as their feet left the solid ground of the United States and moved steadily upward onto the ship. Both men harbored the same thought...it might be a long time before they felt American soil again.

Once they were aboard the Queen Elizabeth and were standing in line for orders and directions to their births, Jack tugged on his friend's shoulder. "Hey, Slick!" he said brightly. Private Burrow hated his given name, Adrian, and, for some reason he failed to explain, insisted that all his friends call him Slick. Jack continued, "I've heard of these cushy ocean liners used by the Vanderbilts and Rockefellers and such. You think we'll get a luxury cabin with a balcony over the ocean, maid service, and someone to bring our meals whenever we ring a bell?"

Slick surveyed the small, drab, grey metal room into which they were crowded along with possibly a thousand other privates. He had watched as thousands had loaded before them, and he knew there were just as many in the line behind them. After a minute's consideration, he said, "I suspect we will get something more in the "economy accommodations" category, but maybe it won't be too bad."

Both men were wrong. With just under twenty thousand men packed onto a vessel designed to carry one tenth as many luxury passengers, all pretext of luxury and even human decency had been cast aside. The men of the 925th found themselves in one of three places during the five day Atlantic crossing. Sometimes they were in the chow line, which was located in a large but poorly ventilated room six decks deep into the bowels of the ship. The food was both good and plentiful, but the rolling decks under their feet made for twenty thousand unsettled stomachs, and good food wasn't much of a priority. One of the most common comments heard in the chow line was, "Do you think I should eat this, or just carry my tray up to the weather deck and throw it in the ocean, which is where it's going to end up anyway?"

When they needed sleep, there were assigned births only for the officers and senior NCOs. Most of the men were on their own, and jostled for a few square feet of space wherever they could find it to unshoulder their packs and lie down. Sleep rarely came, however, because something about lying prone on rolling decks made stomachs churn even more vociferously than when standing. The final, and possibly most essential, place soldiers were found anytime day or night was either at the rail of the weather deck or pushing their way in that direction, seeking a place to throw up where the wind would carry it away rather than blow it back into their own faces.

The huge number of soldiers on board made it impossible for all of them to be vomiting over the rail at the same time, so their steel pot helmets became the standard repository for stomach contents when they were caught below decks. As the crowd permitted, pale faced soldiers would quietly approach the rail and empty the contents from their helmets, dreading the day they had to actually put that thing on their heads.

All things considered, the crossing was a gentle one. The once-stately Queen Elizabeth encountered no rough weather or German submarines, and arrived in Gourock, Scotland right on schedule. The crew of the

Queen numbered almost a thousand men, and most if not all of them, lined the rails smiling and laughing as they watched the pale and red-eyed soldiers shuffle or stagger down the gangway as they disembarked. To a man, they each stopped and stood straighter as they reached the solid planking of the harbor docks. Some actually dropped to their knees and kissed the solid ground at their feet. Luckily, there had been no serious injuries or major illnesses during the crossing, and in only a day or two, every member of the 925th would be fine.

Slick, Jack, and a few others from their platoon had strategically located themselves on the loading deck, and were among the first soldiers to disembark. They walked a hundred yards or so away and finally sat down on a packed dirt street with their backs against the wooden sides of a large warehouse, reveling in the fact that neither the ground nor the warehouse was moving. The men had no way of knowing that they were among more than a million troops transported during the war by the Queen Elizabeth and Queen Mary, most of whom walked these very streets of Gourock after disembarking the liners. The Scottish port had been in service since 1494, but received more passengers during the war years than it had throughout all of its history.

The men were silent for several minutes, watching other soldiers walk slowly by. Finally Slick said, "Guys, when the war is over, if going home means getting on another boat, I'm staying in Europe!"

Gourock was not to be even a temporary home, however. By the end of the day the men were loaded onto yet another train, this one headed south and destined for their permanent home...at least for a few months.

Chapter 7

General Dwight David Eisenhower, Supreme Commander of Allied Forces, sat at the head of the burled oak conference table with a scowl on his face. He headed a very delicate alliance that had decided some months before to plan a massive and secretive assault on Europe designed to drive Hitler's troops back into Germany and contain them there until they could be defeated. He was nearing exhaustion, and the bleak look on his face made apparent to everyone at the table that their comments should be succinct and free from any disagreement. General Sir Bernard Law Montgomery, Commander of the British 8th Army, was speaking in his customary arrogant and tedious manner, and was nearing the end of Ike's patience. A slight, sudden, and brief smile appeared on Eisenhower's face, causing all to notice and even bringing Montgomery to conclude his remarks. All peered at their commander with the question in their eyes.

"General Montgomery mentioned the words that have vexed me since the beginning of this plan," he said with a neutral expression. "Massive, sudden, and secretive. Each of those three adjectives is mutually exclusive of the other two, and yet they describe exactly what we must do. I appreciate each of you traveling here today, for I know you must be as tired as I am with these meticulous planning sessions on top of your burden of command on several different fronts. We are tossing all our eggs into one basket with this plan, so we must..."

The door to the room suddenly burst open and an American Army master sergeant entered. He was a hardened combat veteran of two wars, but he was understandably nervous entering a room filled with so much military brass, so much power.

He looked directly at General Eisenhower. "Sorry to interrupt, sir." Glancing around the room to see all eyes glued to him, the sergeant corrected, "That is, Sirs."

"Yes, Sergeant Lawler, what is it?" Eisenhower asked.

The master sergeant walked briskly toward the head of the table to bend over and speak directly into the supreme commander's ear in such a low tone that no one else could hear. When he finished and stood erect, Eisenhower's face was ashen. The room was cloaked in silence for several minutes as Ike looked down at the stack of papers in front of him, saying nothing. Finally he stood and addressed the group.

"Gentlemen, I have just received word that Colonel Vernon Ambrose, my chief of staff, was shot down while flying here to stand in my stead while I attend other strategic meetings." He was silent for an extended time before saying, "Many of you knew Vern. He was a good friend and a remarkable soldier." He walked toward the door without making eye contact with any of the assemblage, the master sergeant following closely. As Ike reached the door, he turned to his generals with a noticeable shimmer of tears in his eyes and said, "Gentlemen, please continue without me. There are matters to which I must attend. I will return presently."

Ten minutes later Master Sergeant Lawler entered the conference room to summon General Walter Bedell Smith, known as 'Beetle' to his friends. The senior sergeant and lieutenant general walked in silence until they reached Ike's makeshift private office. General Smith had been Eisenhower's chief of staff until the Sicily campaign had demanded so much of his time that Ike had replaced him, at least temporarily, with Colonel Ambrose. General Smith, along with Generals Montgomery, Patton, and Bradley, had all been brought from Sicily to this meeting, hopefully only for a few days. The door to the office was open when Smith arrived.

"Beetle! Come in...come in." The Supreme Commander said more brightly that expected. He pointed to a rickety old straight backed chair and said, "Please have a seat." With a warm and unexpected smile, he continued, "Carefully. It doesn't look as if it will support much weight."

"Sir, I'm very sorry for your loss. I know he was a friend as well as one hell of a chief of staff. Ambrose was an exceptional soldier." General Smith said solemnly.

Ike smiled once more. "That's high praise coming from you, Beetle. Thank you." He paused for a brief moment as the smile vanished. "War has always been hell, not only for the inevitable loss of good men, but also for the fact often we can't even take adequate time to mourn them. Beetle, you are going to be tied up for at least a few more months in Sicily and, hopefully Italy. I can't pull you away to return as my chief of staff. I would like you to find someone else for the job, someone just like yourself, who knows and understands combat, but also understands diplomacy and can handle all the egos and the internal conflicts that seem to constantly arise within this coalition of allies. Obviously I need this man quickly. Surely there is someone in this theater of operations who meets those requirements."

This time it was General Smith who smiled. "I don't have to look, Ike. I know just the man."

"Tell me about him," Eisenhower said, surprised.

"Major Jerald Martin," Beetle answered quickly. "Currently the CO at the Adjutant General School at Fort Jackson. He's quite a story."

"Combat action in Europe?" Eisenhower queried.

"Not in this war," answered Smith with a wry smile. "Martin volunteered as a teenager in 1917. He served with the 3rd Corps until being wounded during the Aisne-Marne campaign. After a couple of months in the hospital he was reassigned to Pershing's 3rd Army, and was wounded again during the Meuse-Argonne offensive. His wounds...head, neck, and left arm, caused some nerve damage and partial paralysis of his left hand. Nothing really bad. He can still use the hand, but a couple of his fingers don't work. His wounds, by the way, were received while he was digging his lieutenant out of a collapsed bunker. The rest of the platoon ran after the bunker was shelled, but Martin stayed behind to dig out the officer...saved his life. He's a brave guy...good guy."

Ike asked, "Was he mustered out due to his wounds?"

"He refused to be invalided out," General Smith said with admiration in his tone. "Stayed with his unit as a company clerk. He apparently was a quick learner, and by the end of the war was working at Division Headquarters."

"And after the war?" Ike prompted.

"You're going to like this, Ike." Smith answered. "After mustering out he got a job working for a congressman in Washington. By 1921 he was assistant chief of staff, and dealt daily with some of the same kind of people in leadership positions that we have to. He was good at his job, but really wanted to get back to the Army. He applied for admission to West Point in 1922 and again in 1924, but was turned down both times. Finally he enrolled at the University of Florida and joined their new ROTC program. Even the ROTC didn't want him because of his partial paralysis, but his Congressman/boss intervened and the program finally accepted him."

Ike was shaking his head. "A bona fide hero and West Point wouldn't take him!" he said, incredulous. "Sometimes I wonder what makes the Army tick."

Beetle laughed. "Right now *you* do, sir. Your tick is louder than anyone else's. Martin was commissioned in 1929, and has served with distinction, in several administrative posts, ever since. He's been CO at the AG school for about a year. It's a pretty boring posting for someone of his abilities, and I'm certain he would jump at the chance to serve with you."

"You mentioned wanting someone just like me," Smith said wryly. "Martin has the combat experience and the administrative ability, but there is one big difference between him and me."

Ike raised his eyebrows in question, prompting Smith to continue, "Everyone in this command knows me as a brusque, cranky old curmudgeon."

Eisenhower nodded with a smile and added, "Or worse."

"Major Martin is a *really* nice guy," Beetle said. "He's friendly and diplomatic in situations where I would be like a bull in a china shop. I suspect that approach might even work better with some of the people you have to deal with."

"It sounds as if Major Martin is my man," Ike said emphatically. "Cut the orders. See if he can be at my London headquarters in..." he looked intently at his calendar, "four days."

Chapter 8

A perfect confluence of events conspired to thrust twenty-year-old farm boy Charlie Bradley onto a world stage. His greatest desire when he had joined the Army was to serve in courageous fashion with his friend, Jack, and to return home to a hero's welcome after the war ended. Charlie envisioned himself leading a charge over rolling hills and conquering fortified positions with the enemy running in terror before his valiant attack.

His dreams evaporated with his posting after basic training. Administrative specialist! he thought to himself with disgust as he looked at the rugged terrain racing by outside the window of the Pullman car. The train was destined for Columbia, South Carolina, at which point Charlie and several companions picked up along the way would travel by bus to Fort Jackson for— he bristled at the thought—Administrative Specialist school. His long legs were cramping from the confined space, and as he wiggled in an attempt to find a comfortable position, the young soldier grimaced.

Charlie's seat mate, a pale, thin, bespectacled young man who had introduced himself simply as Private Ogden, saw the frown and asked, "Is something wrong?"

He thrust his somewhat wadded posting orders at the man and growled, "Administrative Specialist School. I always wanted to be a company clerk when I grew up. All my buddies are going to war, and I get to fight the enemy with a typewriter."

"Yeah!" Private Ogden said with excitement in his tone. "I'm going there, too. I was really afraid I would have to go somewhere awful and get shot at. They tell me company clerks almost *never* get killed. Isn't that great?"

Charlie jerked his orders out of the young private's hand and said disgustedly, "Yeah—great." He turned back to the window and watched as the train passed a series of dilapidated shacks clinging to the side of a narrow Appalachian pass.

Ten days later found the same disgusted look on Charlie's face as he glanced around the room filled with forty young men sitting at identical desks and trying to type on identical typewriters. He turned back to his own typewriter and pecked with his index fingers, "The grey goat jumped over the farmer's fence," for the seventh time.

"Use *all* of your fingers, Private Bradley!" growled a hawk-faced corporal who was in charge of the lesson. "This is typing class, not hunt-and-peck class. Chickens hunt and peck—administrative specialists type!"

The door to the classroom opened and a first lieutenant entered. "Corporal Stevens," he said, looking at hawk-face, "a word, please." The lieutenant looked like the officer version of a company clerk. He was a small man with an almost laughable attempt at a peach fuzz mustache who squinted through his horn-rimmed glasses as though the lenses were not quite enough to correct his vision. He and the corporal spoke in low tones for only a few seconds.

The instructor then turned toward the class and said, "Private Bradley, you may now stop your pecking and accompany Lieutenant Masterson."

Charlie was startled, assuming he had done something—possibly pecking at the typewriter keys—that was against Army policy, and he was about to be reprimanded by the officer. His quick mind took only a moment to rule out that transgression as one worthy of punishment from a commissioned officer. As he gathered his few belongings and placed them into his 'company clerk' satchel, it suddenly occurred to him that this was very similar to the way Jack had been singled out after basic training, and whisked away to some unknown posting—probably one that involved real fighting. Charlie was suddenly excited, and walked quickly to the front of the classroom. Lieutenant Masterson turned without a word and left the room. Charlie followed, closing the door behind him as the rattle of typewriter keys began once more.

"Lieutenant...uh...sir?" Charlie asked tentatively as they walked quickly down the hall. Having never personally spoken to an officer before, his voice wavered as he asked, "Can you tell me what this is all about? Have I done something wrong?"

Masterson was not much older than Charlie. At only five feet, five inches tall, he suffered from a bad case of short man syndrome, and obviously enjoyed his rank superiority over the tall, muscular private. "Major wants to see you," he said with a sneer. "If you're in trouble, it must be something really bad. The major doesn't stoop to speaking with privates." The two walked in silence out another door and across a wide expanse of parade ground until they reached the Company Headquarters building.

Major Jerald Martin was Commanding Officer of the 'company clerk' school, as Charlie derisively thought of it. The educational center was formally known as the U.S. Army Adjutant General School, and trained soldiers in all aspects of Army administration, from supply and logistics to weapons procurement to, yes, company clerks and higher level administrators. Major Martin was sitting at his desk when Charlie entered with the lieutenant. He was a fit looking man in his early forties, with dark hair sprinkled with grey. His brow was wrinkled and a faint pink scar was visible from the corner of his right eye traveling down to his ear. The major's eyes, however, were his most captivating feature. Dark blue pupils were held within a framework of bright eyes that showed great interest and vibrancy, as if the officer was truly interested in all that surrounded him. Charlie was surprised when the man rose to greet him.

Steven Abernathy

"Private Bradley?" the major posed it as a question, even though Charlie's nametag was affixed to his blouse.

"Yes, sir!" Charlie answered with emphasis on the sir, standing at rigid attention as he did so.

"Stand at ease," Major Martin said to him. Then, turning to the lieutenant, he said, "Thank you for bringing the private to me. That will be all. After Lieutenant Masterson had gone, closing the door behind him, the major motioned to a chair near his desk and said, "Private Bradley, please have a seat."

He walked back around his desk and sat down as Charlie took a seat and stared uncomfortably at the officer while sitting on the front half of the chair with his back rigid and straight.

The officer held up a thin folder as he spoke. "I've been looking at your record, Private," he began before pausing with what might have been a slight smirk as he noted Charlie's fearful expression. "You have been with us less than two weeks, and have already made something of a name for yourself." He paused once more, noting that the private had a bead of sweat on his brow.

"A name, sir?" Charlie asked in what was almost a whisper.

Martin laughed. "A good name, Private...a good name." He looked at the folder and continued, "I've been looking through your file. Your record at Fort Leonard Wood is exemplary. Test results, physical skills, weapons skills, leadership assessments...all

62

exceptional. The pre-course evaluation tests you have taken here show the same." He smiled warmly. "It seems you can do just about everything but type."

Charlie looked sheepish. "Yes, sir...I mean no, sir. I've only tried that typing for a few days, but I'm just not getting the hang of it. Is that why I'm here, sir? Because I'm flunking typing?"

There was a knock at the door an instant before it opened and Lieutenant. Masterson entered once more carrying a single sheet of paper, which he placed on the Major's desk. "Here are the private's orders, sir. They only need your signature."

"Thank you, Lieutenant," Major Martin said gruffly, a flash of anger revealing itself in those bright eyes. "We'll be a few more minutes. Please excuse us."

As Lieutenant Masterson slammed the office door a little louder than he probably intended, Martin answered with a chuckle, "No, Private, typing is not the issue." He stood, prompting Charlie to snap to attention. "I have transfer orders for you, Private Bradley. This is a voluntary assignment, and you may choose to stay here and possibly learn to type, but you are needed elsewhere."

"A fighting unit, sir?" Charlie asked with excitement in his voice.

"Well," Masterson answered, continuing to chuckle at the young man's, exuberance, "Certainly closer to the fighting that you are here. It's actually a traveling assignment that will take you to Washington,

D.C., New York, and probably several places in Europe. Interested?"

"Yes sir!" Charlie answered immediately. With raised eyebrows he asked, "But doing what, sir?"

"Sit down, private," the Major ordered. After taking his own seat, he said, "I don't usually explain orders to privates, but this is an unusual case. It's a story that takes a few minutes to explain. General Eisenhower was in Tunisia recently. Part of his staff, his Chief of Staff, in fact, and a couple of others, followed him a day later, flying in a C-47. They were shot down off the coast of France. No survivors." He paused for a moment, staring into Charlie's eyes for a reaction.

"General Eisenhower is involved in some extremely sensitive and timely matters and, while he is doubtlessly grieved by the loss of his friend and Chief of Staff, he also realizes that he cannot afford to be without someone to coordinate his staff, his meetings with allied Generals, and even his dealings with the President and various European leaders. Ike heads an alliance of countries including military and civilian leaders, each with their own problems and sometimes with very big egos, and it's quite a juggling act to hold it all together. He's a truly great leader, but he's forced to delegate a great deal to trusted staffers. Someone, that being his Chief of Staff, has to keep up with all of those delegated duties and keep the General apprised of all that's happening.

"Ike has chosen me to be his next Chief of Staff. I have orders to report to him at his London headquarters three days from now. I'm to bring along whatever staff I feel I'll need and be ready to go to work immediately. Quite frankly, I've no idea what kind of staff I'll need because I don't exactly know what I'll be doing at first. I do, however, have an idea. An idea that will involve you, Private Bradley."

Charlie looked completely perplexed. "Me, sir?" was all he could think to ask.

Martin went on as if he had not heard the question. "General Eisenhower has a staff of around fifty. About half are enlisted men, but the rest are officers of every rank, all the way up to lieutenant general. I'll need to work closely with each of them. They are the staff. I'm the chief of staff, so from Ike's perspective they all answer to me. These men are leaders, planners, policy makers...I can't order them around, and can only direct their activities if they feel they know me and can trust me. I need to develop a working relationship with them, but more important, I need to develop a personal connection, a friendship if you will, so that they know me and I know them at a level that assures mutual trust. I need to accomplish this quickly, and for that I need a special kind of assistance. Are you understanding all of this, Private? Do you have any questions?"

Charlie sat dumbly for a long moment, his mind exploding with disparate thoughts he could not quite formulate into words. Finally he said, "Major Martin...

sir...are you sure the lieutenant brought you the right man? I've only been in the Army a couple of months, and I'm not sure..."

Martin interrupted him with explosive laughter. He wiped a tear from his eye as Charlie looked on in amazement. Finally he said, "Private, I owe you an apology." He picked up Charlie's file and motioned with it toward the enlisted man. "This record is short, but it tells me you may be exactly the man I'm looking for. Let me approach this from a different perspective, and explain to you exactly what I need. Then you'll understand where you fit in.

"For the first few weeks I'll need to know all of General Eisenhower's staff on a pretty personal level...their likes and dislikes, their wives', girlfriends', and kids' names, their hobbies, what they did before the war, and so on. It sounds a little tricky, but once I know some of their personal information, I can make idle chat with them. They'll think better of me for remembering the details, and they'll become more readily receptive to whatever military direction or orders I may give them. Particularly for officers who may outrank me, and I fear there will be many of them, the more personal and friendly I can be, the more receptive they will be to receive orders from an underling, even if they know I'm just a messenger from the commanding general. Do you follow?"

"Sure, sir, I understand that," Charlie answered quickly. "It's a little tricky, but it can be very useful. I used to do something similar back home when we were playing baseball. I'd try to get friendly with one of the opposing team players...talk about girlfriends, cars, or whatever...then try to learn about their pitchers and batters. Which pitchers are more likely to throw curves or fast balls. Which batters can't hit a sinker or a curve. Stuff like that. Then I could pass that info along to our team to, maybe, give us an edge." Suddenly, Charlie stopped talking and blushed. "Sorry, sir, I didn't mean to go on like that. I guess I understand except for what it all has to do with me."

"I think you just confirmed that you're my man, Private," Martin stated with a broad smile. "I can't learn and remember all that information myself in a short period of time. I need someone who can learn it, then teach it to me on an as-needed basis. Sooner or later I will *really* know these people, but initially, I will need to resort to a little subterfuge." Seeing a question in Bradley's eyes, the officer added, "A little trickery, Private."

He leaned forward again for emphasis. "I need *you* to do the same thing you did back home playing baseball. Wherever I go, whomever I meet with the first few weeks and months, I want you standing nearby. If I ask a staffer about his wife or his work before the war, I want you to very discreetly write that information down. I want you to research these people, find out everything you can about them. I want you specifically because as an enlisted man, you will be free to talk informally with all of the enlisted staff. I know that enlisted men tend to know just about everything, both good and bad, about their officers. Write it all down. Make a secret dossier on everyone I, rather we, will work with. When I walk into a room, be able to whisper in my ear who I am meeting, whether or not I have met them before, and if I have, something about their personal life I can bring up to surprise them I would remember such a detail. I need *you* to make *me* look good in front of these new people. I need you to learn all about them without letting them know you are learning all about them. Understand?"

Charlie's eyes lit up. "Like a spy, sir?" he asked excitedly.

The major smiled. "I suppose, in a way. Just remember we're all on the same side." He held up the orders. "Private, these orders are for you to accompany me to England as my assistant. To make your job a little easier, I'm authorizing a field promotion to sergeant for you. It's a big jump, but three stripes will make you look a little more seasoned than you really are and make it a little easier to talk freely with all of the enlisted staff. I suspect you'll learn the ropes very quickly.

"As I explained, this assignment is voluntary. Do you accept the challenge, or would you prefer to stay here and learn to type?"

Charlie didn't have to think about it. He smiled, excitement pouring from his expression, and said, "Sure, sir, I accept. Wow! I'm not sure what else to say." His smile faded and the excitement on his face was replaced with a pensive look. "Can I ask a question, sir?" The officer gave him a slight nod, and Charlie continued, "There must be hundreds of men in the Army who are more qualified for this job than me. Why choose a country boy with an eighth grade education over those people, sir?"

Major Martin looked at him for a long moment, mentally composing his answer. Finally, he said, "We'll be working very closely for hours each day. Do you mind if I call you Charles? Only in private, of course. I'll address you by your rank when others are present."

Charlie nodded. "Sure, sir, but Charlie would be better. Only my mother calls me Charles. That just wouldn't feel right."

Martin laughed. "Okay, Charlie it is. Now to your question, Charlie. You're right. There are hundreds of veteran soldiers out there that could do this job. I started looking from within my command and this school because General Eisenhower more or less required it. Whatever he and the allies are planning, it's huge in scope. Administrative personnel throughout Europe and the United States...those people who are best suited to do the job you just volunteered for...are already taxed to their limits in planning for this event in addition to their day to day duties. Taking even one seasoned clerk or assistant from his duties would put an unnecessary burden on someone else at a very critical time. Ike knows this better than anyone, and he wants me to bring new blood to the table, so to speak."

"Second, the Army teaches you...teaches all of us...to think in a certain way that works best within the military system. As someone new to military service, you haven't been fully indoctrinated into this way of thinking. It's not a bad way, understand, but it closes the mind somewhat to what I call 'out of the box' thinking.

Charlie's eyebrows raised in question as he said, "Sir?"

Major Martin chuckled and answered the private's question with one of his own. "Charlie, do you remember how fifty caliber ammunition is stored in the ammo box?" Seeing a nod from the young private, he continued, "Every round of ammunition is lined up perfectly, as if standing at attention. That's the way the Army wants it. Do you follow me so far?"

Charlie nodded slowly and answered, "Yes sir. I understand...at least I think so."

Martin continued, "That ammunition is in straight and rigid lines inside the box because that's the most efficient way to transport it, and that's what's best for the Army. "Now," he said in a sharper tone, causing Charlie to jump, "imagine taking a hundred rounds out of the ammo box and throwing them on the ground. What would happen?"

"They wouldn't be lined up proper any more. They'd be scattered, pointing in all directions," the young man answered, starting to get the idea but still not knowing where the officer was headed with this example.

"Exactly," the major answered brightly. "If the shells are out of the box they're scattered, no longer rigidly pointing in the same direction. The Army doesn't like that. It wants everything uniform, everything working together, everything pointing the same way. Can you think of any other examples, Charlie?"

"Sure, Sir," the private answered quickly. "Marching in basic training and here at company cler..." he caught himself, "at administrative specialist school." Martin was smiling broadly at the slip as Charlie finished, "We march in straight lines all together. If even one man is out of step, the drill sergeant gets all bent out of shape. I suppose if everyone just lit out in all directions, like the ammo out of the box, he would just have a heart attack."

"You're probably right, Charlie," the major said. "The Army wants its shells all aligned in the same direction, it wants its aircraft to fly in formation, it wants its men to march at attention in straight lines and ranks. There is something else the Army wants, though. Something you might not have thought about."

"What's that, Major?" Charlie asked, now enthralled.

Major Martin did not keep him in suspense. "The Army wants all of its men to think a certain way, to follow a certain philosophy, to accept orders without question and even to anticipate those orders to a large degree. In other words, the Army has created a box for thinking, just like it has a box for ammunition. It wants all of its soldiers to think the same inside that box. The Army really doesn't like free thinkers or people who think outside their box.

"Civilian people...regular people like your friends and relatives back home...tend to think independently. If there is a problem to solve in your hometown and ten different people are asked for ideas how to solve it, you might get ten different answers. The Army isn't like that. If I called in ten sergeants to ask for recommendations on completing a certain task, at least eight of them would give me exactly the same answer." He laughed at himself as he continued, "The other two probably didn't understand the question."

"Charlie, the Army wants all of its soldiers to think alike. It begins this education in basic training, and it will continue throughout your military career. One of the reasons you're particularly suited to my purpose is that you haven't been in the Army very long. Your mind hasn't been completely indoctrinated in that slight corruption. You think the way 'regular people' think in other words, and that may be important in our dealings with civilian personnel who are involved in this project.

"Those are the main reasons I chose you, along with your record of achievement during your short stay in the Army. But as a third reason, just in the short time I have been talking with you, I've learned that you're intelligent, a man who can think quickly, and," the corners of his lips lifted into a slight smile, "you have a slightly devious side to you that will fit our purposes perfectly. In other words, Charlie, you are the ideal man for this job."

Major Martin stood and held out the orders to Charlie. "Pack your duffel, *Sergeant*." He emphasized the change in rank. "We leave the day after tomorrow at oh-five-hundred hours. That is all," he finished formally.

As Sergeant Bradley reached out to open the door, the major said, "And Charlie." Bradley turned back as he concluded, "Thanks for volunteering."

Charlie exited the administration building and walked across the compound in a daze, filled with anticipation, awe, and considerable disbelief in what had just happened. From throwing bales of hay in the Missouri bootheel to working in London, England with General Dwight Eisenhower all in a span of two months. It was almost too much to fathom. He wondered for a moment how Jack was doing. His lifelong friend had simply vanished after going to the CO's office at Fort Leonard Wood. Would the two friends ever meet again?

Chapter 9

Most of the 925th Engineer Aviation Regiment arrived at the Boreham, England airfield on September 7th. The term airfield was a gross misnomer, as the men of the regiment would find out as soon as they disembarked from the train. Even the term 'field' failed to adequately describe the muddy mass of vast expanse that welcomed them. There were no buildings, no air strip, nothing at all on the gently rolling countryside to indicate human habitation. Early rains had been drowning the area for the previous two weeks, and a heavy rain continued as grumbling soldiers trudged from the railcars and began to form ranks for a headcount and immediate orders.

The first order of business was to erect tents that would serve as their temporary quarters and various company and regimental headquarters. The soldiers quickly discovered that some brain dead quartermaster had located the tents at the very back of two boxcars, behind several tons of heavy equipment that required unloading before the canvas shelters could be reached. Three hours of miserable working conditions or, in the case of some who had nothing to do, standing around in the relentless rain waiting for the chance to throw up a shelter, were needed to reach the large stack of folded canvas. When finally removed from the boxcars, the tents went up quickly. Even though they were wet and the ground was ankle deep in mud, the men welcomed the chance to stand out of the rain.

"Welcome to England," someone said in one of the crowded shelters.

"Yeah, welcome," Jack answered as he stood near the open flap and watched the incessant rain. "I guess we'd better put up a tent for the doctors before we all come down with pneumonia and need to be treated."

Crates of C Rations were unloaded and quickly distributed so the men could have a meal, albeit a cold one. Twelve ounces of meat and beans eaten directly from the can would comprise the bulk of their sustenance until a mess tent could be erected, dried out, and equipped.

Before the day was done, wooden flooring had been assembled in most of the tents, finally giving the men a relatively dry environment and a somewhat solid foundation on which to place their cots and duffels. As darkness cloaked the east of England, the exhausted and mostly still damp men of the 925th finally slept with rain pounding on the canvas over their heads.

Morning found the heavy rain gone, replaced by a heavy mist that limited vision to no more than a hundred feet. Occasionally the mist would develop into a fine drizzle, but thankfully it seemed to lack the will to evolve into actual raindrops. Scuttlebutt said the day was to be spent learning to erect a new and more permanent shelter called a Nissen Hut. These new structures would be the permanent barracks for the 925th, and the men were to learn their construction from the ground up. After a C-ration breakfast complete with actual hot coffee, they were assembled by platoons to learn the basics of Nissen Hut assembly.

The huts were simple and ingenious in concept. Floors were made of either concrete poured on site or, as would be the case at Boreham, pre-cut tongue and groove wood nailed to a wooden frame, also pre-cut and ready to assemble. The outside walls were corrugated steel arches, each pre-curved to make one third of a semicircle. Two of the metal arches, on opposite sides of the structure, would be driven into the ground at one end and leaned against a wooden frame. A third section, identical to the first two, would be attached to the arches on either side with a six inch overlap to form the top of the structure. Each metal sheet was just over ten feet in length and two feet, two inches wide. Fifty-four sheets were required to construct a standard sized hut, which when completed was about eighteen feet in length and width, and nine feet tall at the peak of the arch. The ends of the completed half cylinder were framed with 2 X 4 inch lumber and covered with weatherboard. Windows could be placed in the front and back walls. The structure was tightly sealed and could be insulated and heated by a small wood or coal burning stove.

The British Sergeant Major who was briefing Bravo Platoon, which included Jack and several of his friends since their whirlwind training in California, was about to begin explaining with diagrams how a team of four men could erect a Nissen Hut, complete with wooden floor, in one day. He stopped for a moment to watch an Army Air Corps captain walking purposefully toward the platoon. He spoke with the captain in low tones for a few minutes before surrendering his podium, constructed by the simple expedient of throwing down a wooden palate into the mud, to the officer.

"Men," the captain said without taking the time to introduce himself, "it was our hope that our first task in this rather barren wasteland," he motioned around with his right hand as he spoke, "would be to erect permanent quarters and other necessary structures to make this place more fit for human habitation." He paused for effect before continuing, "That is not to be the case, however. Our ultimate mission here is to build a Class A airfield with three concrete runways for what will primarily be B-26 Marauder operations. An emergency situation has developed that requires our immediate action."

"These damnable heavy rains," the officer looked at the sky, which was darkening as he spoke, threatening to open up a new deluge on the exposed men, "have concentrated in an area about a hundred miles west and two hundred miles north of here. That large area just happens to include many of our air fields that mount daily operations against Germany. These airfields are primarily grass strips, and they have become muddy bogs that cannot serve as operational airstrips to handle heavy bomber operations. We have been forced to move several squadrons farther to the north and west to find solid, dry ground to act as runways for their sorties. Problem is, even from our airfields near London and on this southeast coastal area, some of the longer missions tax the aircrafts' fuel reserves to the maximum. Moving the bases of operation west and north makes the distance even farther, and makes it impossible for some important targets to be reached."

Bravo Company listened in silence. The vast majority of the men were privates, and unaccustomed to lengthy explanations from officers, usually responding only to orders handed down the chain of command. They looked around at each other with questions in their eyes, not knowing where this lengthy elucidation would take them. A moment later the captain got to the point of his interruption of their training.

"The 92nd Bombardment Group, consisting of five B-17 squadrons and one B-25, is currently posted at Podington, which is seventy miles northwest of here. Their grass field is too muddied to support operations, so the entire group was moved ten days ago to Glasgow, Scotland. Bombing assignments are handed out weeks in advance, and the 92nd is to fly sorties to Berlin for up to nine days in a row beginning four days from now. Their current temporary base of operations in Scotland is beyond their fuel capacity to reach the German capital and safely return. We need to move the group here as quickly as possible. This base will cut the distance and flying time by almost forty percent, and will make the raids well within the fuel capacity of the B-17s."

"Obviously," said the officer while motioning around at the muddy field, "this field is no better than the 92nd's home in Podington. But Podington does not have the 925th Engineers. Your orders for the next few days are to build a temporary runway and staging area for the 92nd Bombardment Group. You'll be working in steady rain, if the forecasts are correct, and for the foreseeable future you will not be constructing Nissen Huts. I hope your tents are comfortable," he said with a sudden smile.

"Boxcars on the train that brought you here are filled with Marsden mats. I'm told you men can construct a runway two hundred feet wide and five thousand feet long within two days utilizing the mats. To accomplish the task at hand and get the aircraft here to begin their mission on time, I want to alter those dimensions temporarily. The 92nd has flown over two hundred missions and has incurred some attrition, but still has forty eight operational aircraft that will be coming here. We'll need a five thousand foot runway, but the width can be held down to a hundred feet, which will make construction go much faster. Along with the runway, we'll need a staging area of Marsden mats large enough to park the forty eight B-17s and another eight or ten ancillary aircraft and trucks for transporting ordinance and fuel."

After looking intently at the men in silence for a long moment, he concluded, "You will begin work immediately. I expect a completed Runway 18/36 and a staging area by day after tomorrow. Unless we are socked in with fog, three squadrons from the 92nd will be landing here late in the afternoon. They'll be arriving directly from a bombing mission to Dresden, Germany. There will be around fifty aircraft and crews, less any attrition from the mission. They will be shot up, tired, and wounded. Podington will be sending several trucks with medical supplies and personnel, aircraft parts and technicians, and ordinance for their next missions. We need to be ready for them as well as the aircraft. I want two squads working with Sergeant Major Collins to erect four Nissen huts at the edge of what will be the staging area. These will serve as hospitals, shelter for the tired crews, and any dry storage that may be required for aircraft parts or ordinance. The rest of you, along with several other platoons will be tasked with assembling the Marsden mats into a runway and staging area." He stopped for a moment and looked over the group once more. "That is all for now. This is what you trained for. Get to work and get it done."

The captain spoke with Sergeant Major Collins for a few moments before walking away. As if on cue, a cold rain began pelting the men as they stood waiting for their individual assignments.

Chapter 10

Jack stood at the edge of the staging area, which in this case was simply a giant parking lot with a few buildings scattered around the edges, along with the rest of Bravo Platoon, watching the flight of bombers in the distance as they broke formation to enter the landing pattern of the newly completed Boreham runway. Construction had been finished only hours before. The steel mats were usually assembled on top of a hard surface that had been graded flat and often fortified with gravel before the runway panels went down. There had been no time to place gravel or other suitable base material on the wet ground, so the Marsden mats had been assembled directly on top of the thick mud. The men were all anxious to see how the runway held up under the weight of a landing B-17.

Several of the engineers had noted, "It's a little squishy," when first walking on the steel surface. The mats were each ten feet long, but only fifteen inches wide. They were designed in such a way that identical mats could be attached on any side, making a hard surface that was flexible at the joints. With only mud beneath the mats, they were *very* flexible. When time and conditions permitted, the mats would be extended to form a runway two hundred feet wide, and would then serve as reinforcing structure for a poured concrete runway to provide a stable surface for any conditions. For now, none of that was possible, so the men of the 925th had done the very best job they could under the circumstances. Currently, each of them stood by, many with fingers crossed, some praying, hoping their very best was good enough to land the bombers safely.

Every member of Bravo Platoon held his breath as the first bomber flared for touchdown at the end of the new runway. It was a B-25. Not quite as heavy as the four engine B-17, it was still a good test of the stability of the runway. The main gears touched and began to roll relatively smoothly, allowing the pilot to bring down the nose wheel after the craft had slowed to a suitable speed. The first aircraft of the 92nd Bomb Group taxied onto the large staging mat and was directed to a parking spot. Other B-17s were in line for a long succession of landings. The Marsden mats covering the English bog performed magnificently and forty-four aircraft landed safely. Five B-17s and crews had been lost during the mission. Many of the landing bombers were riddled with bullet holes. Four had lost an engine. Over half of the crews had incurred injuries and deaths from within their numbers.

Medical and support staff from the 92nd had not yet arrived at Boreham. The engineers had two physicians and a small nursing staff, all of whom were immediately pressed into service to treat the wounded airmen. Bravo Platoon was assigned to act as litter bearers and perform any other task needed to see to the care and comfort of the battered and exhausted crews.

The last B-17 to land had trailed the rest of the group by at least ten miles. A trail of dark smoke could be seen coming from its port wing while still two or three miles out. As the craft neared the runway, onlookers were aghast to see at least four feet of the port wing was missing and the outboard engine was heavily smoking as if it might be on fire. It was obvious from the yawing back and forth that the pilot was having great difficulty controlling the crippled bomber, but was making a valiant effort to keep the nose centered on the runway. At the last, the aircraft touched down very hard, causing the Marsden mats to buckle in a hole at least three feet deep. The helpless onlookers froze in terror as the Flying Fortress literally sank into the ground at the far end of the runway. Scant seconds later, however, the craft clumsily shot back into the air, then settled down into a much softer landing. It rolled about twenty five hundred feet and stopped in the middle of the runway.

Flight crews started running toward the craft, prompting Jack and several other members of his platoon to follow suit. They quickly found that the entire crew was alive, but eight of the ten had been wounded, four very seriously. The two uninjured crewmen were attempting to hold compresses on the heavily bleeding wounds of three crewmen. The pilot had a serious head wound, and was deliriously barking nonsensical orders and attempting to fly the airplane even though it was at a dead stop. The copilot was unconscious, with a large piece of the starboard window protruding from the right side of his neck. A few of the men took a second to wonder who had landed the airplane and how, but they left those questions for now to turn all their attention to helping the crew.

As the wounded airmen were helped or handed out of the bomber, members of Bravo Platoon were waiting with litters and jeeps to transport them to the makeshift hospital. Jack carefully placed one end of his litter, on which lay the copilot, Lieutenant John Morgan, onto the back of a waiting Jeep. The large piece of quarter inch thick Plexiglas was still sticking out of his neck, and the men had been advised not to attempt to remove it until the lieutenant was at the hospital. Jack climbed into the Jeep to hold the officer's head and prevent any movement from displacing the glass. As the jeep crept down the runway toward the Nissen huts, Lieutenant Morgan's eyes opened. Jack felt tension on his hands as the wounded man tried to move his head.

"Don't try to move, sir," Jack said, increasing the pressure on the sides of Morgan's head. "You're wounded, but you're going to be okay."

"Where am I?" asked the officer.

Jack smiled. "On the ground, sir...you're on the ground."

When the story was finally pieced together, it was nothing short of amazing. The flight had encountered fighter aircraft over the target. Several in the formation were seriously damaged, and twenty-seven crewmen lost their lives. The pilot of Lieutenant Morgan's B-17 was wounded in the head, but was conscious throughout the flight and in a crazed condition that made it impossible for him to fly the craft. Lieutenant Morgan, while bleeding from a neck wound, fought off the delirious captain with his left hand while flying the Fortress with his right. There was no help to be had, because the uninjured crewmen in the back were busy caring for the seriously wounded. To make matters worse, a large portion of the port wing had been shot away, and the outboard port engine had been destroyed. The wounded lieutenant fought off the crazed pilot for two hours as he flew his seriously crippled aircraft to a landing at Boreham.

First Lieutenant John C. Morgan was later awarded the Medal of Honor for his actions during this flight.

Over the next few days more aircraft arrived from Podington along with the complete complement of support staff and equipment. Daily life was settling into a routine of building a permanent camp for the engineers and preparing for the next bombing missions for the air crews. Replacements for the bomb group were slow in coming, both airplanes and men, and the commanding officer was understandably concerned about his ability to assemble an adequate force from the remnants he currently had available. Aircraft were being repaired. Pilots were in short supply, but that could be managed. There were several excellent copilots available who could pilot the aircraft if necessary, and in extreme circumstances many of the flight engineers were familiar enough with the controls of the B-17 to serve as copilot. The problem was gunnery crew. Far too many had been wounded or killed during recent missions, and replacements had not yet come. Daylight bombing missions were very risky at best, and high casualty counts were expected, but flying to a distant target without adequate guns to protect against enemy fighters was simply suicide. It could not be done.

About the same time the air group commander was considering his crew problem, Jack and a few other engineers were carrying extra Marsden mats from the rail platform where they had been unloaded to a distant part of the staging area, so they would be readily available for necessary repairs. The mats weighed only sixty six pounds each, and could easily be carried by one man. Some of the bigger guys even carried one under each arm, just to prove they could. Normally a simple task, carrying the ten foot by fifteen inch steel mat while slogging through ankle deep mud caused heavy breathing among even the strongest and fittest. When Jack reached the edge of the staging area and found sound footing on the assembled mats, he put down his load and took a minute to flex his leg muscles and enjoy the freedom of movement without having to extricate each step from the deep, sucking, mud. He was about to pick up his mat and continue to the storage point when he noticed a familiar figure walking toward him. Jack snapped to attention and gave a crisp salute as Lieutenant Morgan approached, looking healthy but sporting a thick bandage around his neck that extended past his collar and into his flight jacket.

Lieutenant Morgan returned the salute and immediately said, "At ease, soldier." He smiled broadly and continued, "You're the man who helped me out of the Fortress and into the hospital, aren't you?"

"Well, sir, I was one of several, I guess," Jack answered. "As I heard the story, you are quite a hero, sir. I'm proud I was able to help out in just a little way. You really did a good job flying that plane while holding your captain away from the steering yoke for two hours, then landing safely on a runway that was near collapse. You saved all their lives, sir. If they asked me, I'd say they should give you a medal."

The lieutenant looked embarrassed. "To tell you the truth, Private, I was scared to death. I remember flying back, fighting the shot up wing and the dead engine, and I remember trying to hold back Captain Willis. There wasn't much holding us in the air, and the captain was in such a state that if he had taken control and jerked us around like we were a P-51 Mustang, we would have stalled and spun out." The young man, who couldn't have been more that two or three years older that Jack, looked pensive for a long moment before saying, "I've tried, but I don't remember the landing at all. I'm totally blank. I guess I was running on automatic. Thanks for your kind words, however. I don't know about any medal, but I'm glad to be on the ground in one piece." He brushed his fingertips against his bandaged neck and continued, "Come to think of it, I guess I came back with an extra piece."

"How is your captain, sir," Jack asked, "and the rest of the crew?"

"Captain Willis was shipped out to a London hospital this morning. He was still pretty delirious when I last saw him. The docs here say they don't know enough about brain injuries, but there are specialists in London. The rest are doing pretty well, I guess. Jimmy Kent, one of our waist gunners, is still touch and go. He was sent to London, too. The rest are going to pull through, but will be out of action for a good while."

Jack thought to brag on himself a little. "I volunteered for gunnery school back in basic. Even had my orders, but at the last minute I was assigned to this engineering regiment." He looked into the sky with craving in his eyes. "I sure wanted to be a gunner, though, and would have been good at it. I was actually able to go on three training missions while we were in California...two of them in B-17s. Crew chief said I was a better shot than some of their trainees who had been through the whole training course."

The private hung his head for a moment and said softly, "I know we shouldn't be wishful of going to combat and maybe killing other people," he started, then raised his head, eyes bright, and finished, "but when I had that big ole' fifty caliber in my hands shootin' down those targets, it sure seemed like that was the right thing for me." He bent down to pick up his mat. "Sure would beat sloggin' around in the mud and rain carrying Marsden mats from one place to another."

Jack looked back at the Lieutenant, regret on his face. "Sorry, sir," he said, "I'm not a complainer, and I didn't mean to go on like that."

The young officer was looking at Jack with raised eyebrows conveying both a surprised and thoughtful expression. "That's okay, Private," he started, "don't worry about it. So you have had a little gunnery experience?"

"Yes, sir!" Jack answered proudly. "I scored seventy two out of one hundred on my first training flight as waist gunner...almost ninety on the second!"

"Ninety percent from a waist gun position?" the officer asked, incredulous. "That's..." he started to say impossible, but didn't want to offend the private, who seemed very proud of his accomplishment, "incredible." He looked over his shoulder toward the hospital hut. "I've got a good crew, but none of them even comes close to ninety percent accuracy, particularly at the waist. Things are a lot different in actual combat, but even so..." He let the thought drift away as Jack balanced the ten foot steel mat in his arms.

"Sir, I've enjoyed talking to you," Jack began, "but I guess I'd better..."

"What is your unit assignment, Private?" Morgan asked.

"Charlie Company, Bravo Platoon, sir," Jack answered, then pointed off into the distance. "Headquartered about a quarter of a mile over that way."

"Are you aware of any other members of your company who had any gunnery training?" the officer asked.

Jack thought for a moment, finally answering with a grin, "Sir, most of the guys don't want any part of combat if they can help it. I can't say I blame them. It's a good way to get killed, I hear. But there were a few of us in engineering school who tried to spend as much time as we could around the flight training units just hoping for a chance to go up and shoot the fifties."

Morgan indicated toward the hospital with a tip of his head, wincing as the movement pinched the neck wound. "Some of the guys over in the hospital have been with the captain and me for more than twenty missions. A couple of them have more than enough to qualify them to rotate home, but they won't go. We get very close, with all those combat missions, is what I am saying. Most of the crewmen I call by their first names...I'm just more comfortable doing that, and the men prefer it, too. Most of the Flying Fortress crews I know are the same way. There's only ten of us in the aircraft, and we're more like a family than anything else."

He looked intently at Jack, "Do you mind if I call you by your first name, Private."

Jack was more than a little confused. "No sir," he said. "It's Jack...sir."

"Thanks, Jack," Lieutenant Morgan said. "I should let you get back to work, but I suspect you'll hear from me soon. I have an idea."

Not knowing how, or even whether he should answer, Jack put down his load once more, came to attention, and gave the lieutenant a sharp salute. He held the salute until the officer answered it, then both men went on their way.

Jack picked up his Marsden mat and began to walk toward the delivery point, unaware that he had just volunteered to be a waist gunner on the next several bombing missions deep into Germany. Lieutenant Morgan's Fortress had been dubbed "Hitler's Headache" by its original crew over a year ago. While other of the B-17 squadron had painted logos on their fuselages depicting beautiful blonds, birds in flight, or cartoon characters, "Hitler's Headache" sported a painting of the German dictator with a B-17 dropping a bomb onto his head. Jack would soon be the aircraft's newest crewman.

Chapter 11

Jack strained to hear the flight engineer, First Lieutenant William "Billy" Holland, as he shouted over the din of the four twelve hundred horsepower Wright Cyclone engines while they strained under full power to claw their way through sky up to twenty five thousand feet. The private was already uncomfortable, even though the Fortress had lifted off the runway only a few minutes before. It was his first combat mission, and he could already tell it was going to be a far different experience than the training flights he had taken in California. Those flights had been at low altitude, shooting at stationary targets erected on the sides of low mountains. The outside air was always warm then, and, of course, the stationary targets did not shoot back.

Jack's current discomfort was from the several layers of heavily insulated clothing he had been instructed to don before boarding the Flying Fortress. The outside was humid and the temperature was in the forties on the ground, so it took only minutes to begin sweating heavily. He unsnapped and opened as much of the heavy uniform as possible, knowing it was dangerous to sweat because the layer of moisture against his skin would freeze when they reached high altitude and cause all manner of problems. The private knew he would add additional layers to the already heavy uniform, including a flack vest, full face oxygen mask and radio mike, heavy gloves, and several layers of head covering and earphones for communication, before the aircraft reached cruising altitude, but for now he would remain as well ventilated as possible. The squadron would fly in formation at twenty five thousand feet, an altitude where there was not enough oxygen to sustain life, and where the temperature inside the unpressurized, uninsulated fuselage sometime dropped as low as minus sixty degrees Fahrenheit.

"Private!" the flight engineer shouted over the din. "Come on back to the port waist gun with me." The two men, along with all of the other gunners, had assembled in the radio room for takeoff. It was standard procedure, as the radio room was forward of the belly turret and thus in a stable part of the aircraft. After takeoff, the airmen would move back to their gunnery positions and prepare for the high altitude flight by hooking up their oxygen lines and putting on the rest of their flight gear. The lieutenant helped Jack put on his flack jacket and shouted instructions to him. "It's going to be very cold...killing cold...when we get to cruising altitude. If you start to feel a burning sensation anywhere around your mask or on your neck, get another crewman to check you. Any exposed skin will get frostbite quickly, and that can be a real problem. Don't take any chances." He moved to the gun. "Couple things you need to remember as you fire the 'fifty'. First," he held up part of the long ammunition belt, "if you pull the trigger and hold it, this ammo belt represents three minutes of firing. Three minutes!" he emphasized. "That's all you've got for the whole mission, so don't waste your ammo. Shoot in short bursts, and make them count. Second thing to remember and this is very important," he waved his arm toward a nearby B-17 flying in their formation. "There are other aircraft and crews out there, not very far away. Don't shoot them. They will have their hands full fighting the Germans, and don't want to dodge your bullets. It sounds funny, but almost every mission one or more of our planes takes friendly fire. I hear you're a good shot, so don't let it happen from your gun."

The lieutenant stopped for a moment, looking grim. "There's a third thing you need to know. In about an hour we'll begin to encounter the first wave of fighters. It will be utter chaos when they first start shooting. You will be cold and miserable; your joints will be stiff from the freezing temp and the confined space. Suddenly, we will be in a battle the likes of which you can't even image. Crewmen next to you may be shot and bleeding, one of the Fortresses you can see out the window may explode, or spin out to the ground. It hasn't happened to me yet, but our own craft may be disabled to the point that we have to throw on our chutes and bail out...keep that in the back of your mind and be ready should it ever happen."

Jack looked at the officer with wide eyes.

"The first four or five minutes are the worst. You will feel utter terror, you will feel as if you need to curl up in a ball and scream. After those first few minutes, it gets better. You're not any safer and the German fighters don't let up, it's just that you get numb, you go into a kind of shock, you switch to running on automatic pilot and you do your job mechanically. Trust me. I've been through it eighteen times, and it's always the same." He placed his hand on Jack's shoulder. "You'll do fine, Private. Just steel yourself for those first five minutes."

"Okay, sir," Jack said weakly. His stomach already queasy and apparently going into shock just from listening to the officer's lecture.

"There's more," said the lieutenant as he looked down at the large watch strapped around the thick wrist of his insulated flight suit. "As we near the target, the Germans will pull away. Your gunnery job, at that point, will more than likely be finished. The enemy planes don't leave because we have scared them off; they leave because they don't want to be shot down by the German anti-aircraft guns that will begin pelting us. Ack-ack will be exploding all around us—hundreds of shells. In some ways, it's worse than the fighter attacks because we are helpless to do anything about it. It's just pure luck at that point. We either get hit or we don't. There's nothing you can do but hold on tight to something or the concussions from the shelling will knock you all around the cabin." He smiled and patted his chest. "I've broken six ribs so far, and I have plenty to hang onto in my perch under the turret." Jack grimaced and absently patted his own chest as if to be certain it was still intact.

The lieutenant continued, "Once we leave the target area, it's smooth sailing. That is, if the aircraft is intact, if most of the engines are running, if not too much wing surface has been blown away, if our fuel tanks don't have holes in them, if the pilot is healthy and can control the crippled plane, it's smooth sailing all the way. Sometimes the fighters attack us again on the return trip, just for spite, I think. But usually they don't. We don't have any bombs to drop on the way back, and they're happy with all the damage they inflicted on the way in."

"That's it, Private," he said brightly. "Any questions?"

Jack just shook his head, already frightened beyond the ability to speak. He reminded himself that he had asked for this, had applied for gunnery school way back in basic training. That time seemed so long ago, and it was hard to believe it had been only a few weeks. Now he was facing death at the hands of an enemy at five miles above the earth, an altitude where he could as easily die from the cold or lack of oxygen as from a bullet. He thought of his parents, his little brother and sisters, his buddies on the Campbell Chicks baseball team. He wanted all of them to think well of him if he died, so he would force himself to fight bravely and, if necessary, to die bravely. What had happened to Charlie, Jack wondered. He smiled briefly as he suddenly remembered the disgust his friend had expressed on learning he was to be a company clerk. How would Charlie react to this kind of terror? Jack hoped his friend was safe, tucked securely behind a typewriter in some company headquarters far behind the front lines. One of them needed to survive this war.

The lieutenant patted the young airman's shoulder once more. "You'll do fine, Private. All these other guys have gone through it. They'll be just as scared as you are. Me, too." He smiled once more, "I hide my head up in that turret so you guys can't see the fear on my face. Wouldn't do for you to know that the officers are as scared as you are." The flight engineer laughed, at least as well as one can through a plastic oxygen mask and a half dozen layers of woolen scarves tied around the neck. "We'll all do fine; we'll all do our jobs." He turned. "I need to get back to my turret, but you can reach me by radio if you have a question." He walked away, leaving Jack with his own thoughts.

The starboard waist gunner, who Jack knew only as Freddy, was a few feet away. He shouted, "It's bad, Jack, but maybe not as bad as he makes it sound. By the time we get there, we'll all be so addled by this engine noise and the cold that a few ME-109s won't be much more than a bother." He smiled broadly, bringing Jack a little comfort and slowing his heart rate back to near normal, if only for a little while.

An hour and seventeen minutes later, Lieutenant Holland shouted over the radio, "Here they come! Three o'clock high."

Three o'clock was on the starboard side of the airplane, so Jack couldn't see the approaching enemy from his port window. He took a brief moment to step across the fuselage and look through Freddy's window. His breath caught as he saw a cloud of approaching aircraft, too many to count. He stepped back to his gun and readied himself for the attack. There was no fighter escort on this mission, and the squadrons had formed into eighteen-aircraft "Javelin Down" combat boxes, a tactical formation developed by Colonel Curtis LeMay to provide maximum massed firepower for the squadrons' defense.

Jack crouched at his window, his gun pointed upward. His B-17 was one of the high elements of the combat box so there were no friendly aircraft above him. He was free to shoot anything that appeared. Seconds later, a Messerschmitt streaked over the top of his aircraft, its guns already blazing at one of the lower Fortresses in the formation. Jack was nervous, but ready as the enemy appeared. He pulled the trigger for a three-shot burst, aimed at the center of the cross formed by the wings and fuselage of the fighter. After pausing only a second, he pulled the trigger for another burst, but as he pulled, the ME-109 exploded into dozens of pieces and fell from the sky.

"Damn, Jack!" he heard Lieutenant Holland shout. "They said you were a good shot, but...damn!" Guns began rattling from all parts of the aircraft, making any additional communication impossible. The fighters' broke formation, and were darting in and around the B-17's defensive formations, trying to gain tactical advantage against their foe with their speed and maneuverability. The German fighters were fast and nimble, but the amazing firepower of the LeMay formation did much to keep them at bay. Thirty minutes later the attack was over. Not one aircraft was lost from Jack's group formation, although he had watched in horror as two Fortresses spiraled to the ground from distant formations. Jack saw a few parachutes open, but not nearly enough. During the attack, the rookie gunner shot down three ME-109s and disabled another, causing it to leave the fight trailing black smoke from its engine.

"Fifteen minutes to target," the pilot announced. "Get ready for anti-aircraft fire."

Jack watched the other crewmen as they either sat down or stood holding on to parts of the aircraft frame. He sat on the small bench next to his gun, his back resting on the metal skin of the fuselage.

"Don't put your back against the skin," Freddie shouted. "If ack-ack explodes nearby, the concussion will pop that skin in a foot or more and break your back. If you lean against anything, make it the framing. Even that heavy metal will flex a little, but not enough to hurt you."

"Thanks," Jack hollered over the din.

"Main thing is," Freddie continued to shout, "if you know how to pray, pray hard. That's the only defense we have against ack-ack."

Jack nodded, and immediately bowed his head. Prayers didn't seem to come to him, but he began to hear in his mind a song he remembered from when his mother had taken him to church as a boy. *Amazing Grace, how sweet the sound*...at some point he must have begun singing the words through his open mike, for within seconds other voices joined in. Amazing Grace was to become Jack's favorite song for the rest of his life.

Minutes later they were engulfed by anti-aircraft fire. The explosions were all around them, sounding like Fourth of July fireworks in the distance, but becoming deafening as they came closer. The nearest ones jolted the aircraft from all sides, occasionally making the crew feel as if they were on a terrifying rollercoaster ride. Lieutenant Holland held on as he kept his head in the thick Plexiglas turret atop the Fortress. There was nothing at which to shoot, but part of his job was to keep track of engine performance and any damage to the craft, and he could survey most of the outside surfaces from his perch. Jack was amazed that the pilot could keep them on track toward the target while being violently buffeted about by the incessant anti-aircraft shells.

"Target coming up...fifteen seconds," Jack heard the pilot say over the radio.

"Roger," answered the bombardier. "Bomb bays are open. Bombs away in ten...nine..." Jack thought to stand up and watch the bombing from his window, but a nearby explosion jolted the entire aircraft and made him reconsider. He stayed in his seat and attempted to pray.

With a sigh of relief, Jack realized the ack-ack was behind them. The formation made a slow, sweeping turn to the north and then the west, keeping miles between them and the anti-aircraft guns, and began the return trip to England. Damage assessment revealed a few bullet holes through the fuselage that had hit neither crew members nor any vital flight systems. The only casualties were the nerves of the young crew, but that was the case for every mission. As Jack watched, the belly gunner rotated his twin guns until they pointed downward. The maneuver exposed the tiny rectangular door of the cramped belly turret to the inside of the fuselage, and allowed the small man to wriggle from the Plexiglas ball into the cabin with his crewmates. Jack marveled that the man could fold himself into such a tiny ball when within the turret, then unravel himself to exit through the door, all the while wearing the many layers of insulated clothing required to keep from freezing to death. As soon as he had extricated himself from the sphere, the gunner rotated the guns to landing position, then sat down on the floor and began to shake violently. Jack started to move toward him, but stopped when Freddie held out a hand.

"He's okay, Jack. We all get the shakes after a mission." His pale face and slight smile were just visible through the foggy plastic shield of his oxygen mask. "This is a tough way to make a living, you know."

Jack was about to answer, but was suddenly overcome with his own bout of tremors. Seconds later, a river of tears joined the tremors. He held his head down, ashamed of the fact that he was crying uncontrollably, unaware of several other crew members were experiencing the same release of post-combat stress. It was, in fact, a tough way to make a living.

Chapter 12

Charlie and Major Martin arrived in London on schedule, but didn't meet General Eisenhower for a week. The Supreme Commander left word that he would be in New York and Washington, and his new Chief of Staff should settle in and introduce himself to as many as possible. Even though Martin was the Chief of Staff, he picked out an empty desk in the large room that had once been an elaborate hotel ballroom, but now served as workspace for the staff pool, with more than twenty desks arranged throughout the room. Most of the desks were occupied by enlisted men or lower ranking officers. Martin had been promoted to lieutenant colonel for his new job, and found he was the highest ranking officer in the room. Charlie didn't have a desk, but that suited him just fine. He spent most of the first few days moving around the room and meeting the enlisted people. He openly took notes, explaining to each of them that he was jotting down their name and duties to help the new Chief of Staff understand the command structure that currently existed. At the same time, he was surreptitiously recording personal information, the kind Colonel Martin wanted. Charlie would speak to some of the officers later, but for now he plied the enlisted men with questions about the commissioned staff.

Lieutenant Colonel Martin spent the week meeting as many of the officers as he could, always with Charlie lurking unobtrusively in the background, listening to every word. Charlie proved to have a masterful touch at espionage, and within just a few days had assembled beginning dossiers on all but the highest ranking officers. He was quickly accepted by the entire headquarters staff as Colonel Martin's right hand man. One officer summed up the relationship by saying, "It's as if Colonel Martin and Sergeant Bradley are joined at the hip."

The two men devised a precisely choreographed system by which the officer would enter a room or another staffer's office with Charlie several steps behind. If Charlie had not previously briefed him on who he was meeting, the sergeant would quickly approach as Martin entered the room and, after excusing the interruption, present the officer with a note card and say, "Sir, I thought you should see this immediately." If he needed to present more information than could be written on a small card, he would present his boss with a full sheet of paper and say, "Sir, could you please sign this?" Martin would then carefully read the information, sign the paper, and return it to the sergeant. Bradley would take it from the room, but quickly return in case he needed to memorize or record any new information. It was a good system, and both men were able to form working relationships and the beginnings of friendships with many of the staff by the time General Eisenhower returned to London from his strategy sessions in the United States.

When Eisenhower returned, his first order of business was to summon his new chief of staff. Lieutenant Colonel Martin was understandably nervous as he entered the general's office, but Ike quickly put him at ease. He arose when Martin entered and walked around his desk to meet the new man and shake his hand. He even said, "Good morning, Colonel. I'm General Eisenhower," as if there was an Allied soldier anywhere in the world who would not recognize the Supreme Commander of Allied Forces.

Martin met the general's broad smile with his own. "I'm very pleased to meet you, sir," he said. "I want to thank you for this assignment. I hope I can be everything you need. You will certainly get one hundred percent effort from me, sir."

"Take a seat, Colonel," Ike said as he motioned to a pair of plush chairs on one side of his large office. The general took the other chair and continued, "And don't thank me until you've been here a while. I've seen your record. It's impressive. Not many men have your combat experience and also your administrative and diplomatic skills. You've been in some very tough spots as a soldier, but none, I fear, as tough as what you will face here." He suddenly flashed his trademark broad smile once more and asked, "Shall I go on, or do you have that one man staff of yours I've heard about already filling out your request for transfer to more a more reasonable post?"

Martin laughed. "No sir...no transfer request just yet. If you already know of Charlie, that is, Sergeant Bradley, then you probably realize he's off somewhere researching Mrs. Eisenhower's favorite color."

Eisenhower broke into a loud laugh. After a few seconds he said through the laughter, "Eggshell blue, Colonel. Tell him eggshell blue to save him some time. I would like to meet your man as soon as possible, but not just now." He became very serious, reaching to retrieve a folder from a leather satchel at his feet. Martin noticed immediately that the folder was labeled TOP SECRET.

"We're undergoing a name change," he started, motioning all around. "This headquarters is new, and will house SHAEF, which is Supreme Headquarters Allied Expeditionary Force. At this precise moment I command the Mediterranean Theater of Operations from Allied Forces Headquarters (AFHQ) in Algiers. Most of my field commanders receive their orders from that headquarters. That is about to change."

He shifted in his chair. "We're not completely operational yet, but will be within another six to eight weeks. I've spent much of the last two months traveling between Algeria, England, and the United States juggling all the elements of the command transfer." Ike offered a grim smile. "I may be Supreme Allied Commander, but that doesn't mean I don't have to take suggestions from those above me who might desire to run the European campaign. Churchill, President Roosevelt, even the King of England. All want to have input, and rightfully so. The current problem is that I alone am the collection point for all of this nonmilitary input, and the demands it makes on my time take much away from the important task of mounting what will be the largest force ever assembled on the European continent to push the German army out of France and, hopefully, out of existence."

The telephone on Ike's desk rang, and the general moved across the room to answer it. He listened for a moment before answering, "Thank you, Nigel. I'll be there in just a moment."

He returned to take the TOP SECRET folder from the arm of his chair and hand it to Colonel Martin. "I have a meeting scheduled with General Smith in his office." Smiling warmly, he added, "Beetle is the one who recommended you for this position. Did you know that?"

"No, Sir." Martin answered with genuine surprise. "I've never met General Smith. How did he know of me, I wonder?"

"You have impressed many people along the way, Colonel. Keep up the good work." Eisenhower indicated the folder. "Operation Overlord," he said simply. "The plan to invade Europe. The operational plan is not complete, of course, but it is slowly coming together. SHAEF will command three Army groups which, in turn, will command eight armies...close to a million and a half men."

Martin's eyes widened in surprise at the enormity of the operation.

"Study that file here in my office, then lock it in my desk." Ike handed the Colonel a small key. "We'll discuss it in detail this evening." His face brightened and the trademark smile returned. "I'm happy you're here, Colonel, and I look forward to working with you."

Without awaiting a reply, the Supreme Allied Commander turned and left the room, leaving his new Chief of Staff to open the file on Operation Overlord and begin to read.

**

Staff Sergeant Michael Collins picked up a pen and jotted down a note. He had been listening through the open door to the conversation between the supreme commander and his new chief of staff. This was not unusual, because the sergeant was a trusted member of the SHAEF, or, rather, soon to be SHAEF, staff. He was technically a member of General Sir Bernard Law Montgomery's staff, but had been secunded to Ike's staff to act as a low-level intermediary between Eisenhower and Montgomery. Collins and three other enlisted men occupied an office attached to General Eisenhower's, serving primarily as messengers to any other element of the large command when speed of delivery was of prime importance. Collins had been a member of Montgomery's staff since the war began, and even Ike understood that the sergeant was basically Montgomery's spy, with orders to report to the Brit everything of importance that happened at Supreme HQ without regard to its importance to Montgomery's command.

But Sergeant Collins had a secret. He was a spy for Germany as well as for General Montgomery. Born in 1919 during the height of the Irish war for independence, the sergeant had been named after the Michael Collins who was one of the revolutionary leaders and was a distant cousin to the branch of the Collins family to which his namesake was born. Both of the younger Michael's parents and his older sister had been killed by a British bomb near the end of the war in 1921. Michael had survived only because he was asleep in an adjacent room that received only minor damage from the explosion. He had been raised by his father's brother, himself a revolutionary who hated the British. Young Michael was brought up to hate everything British as well, and from a young age was obsessed with avenging the death of his family.

Hitler's Abwer, the intelligence arm of his Ministry of Defense, knew of the enmity many of the Irish felt against the British, and sent numerous agents to both Ireland and England in an effort to capitalize on that hatred by turning as many as possible into covert agents for Germany. The Abwer was headed by Admiral Wilhelm Canaris, a devious man in his own right, who knew the value of spies in the enemy camp and was expert in all of the ways to turn them to his own ends.

Agents had approached Collins, then a Lance Corporal in the British Army, in 1938, knowing he had just been assigned to Montgomery's staff. The war had not yet begun, but Canaris knew it was only a matter of time, and a short one at that. He was in the midst of reorganizing the Abwer to an efficient wartime intelligence gathering organization, and was expanding his network of spies throughout Europe. Collins was an easy mark. The man had actually joined the British army in hopes of finding ways to sabotage operations or do anything possible to disrupt England's military or government operations. He was a patient man, and knew he would have to search carefully for opportunities, then act when he knew he could inflict damage while remaining an enemy unknown to his victims.

Collins had jumped at the chance to work with the Abwer, realizing the organization represented his best opportunity to cripple the British Empire, particularly if the war predicted by his recruiter actually came to pass. When the sergeant was later transferred to Eisenhower's staff, Admiral Canaris began to take special interest in his most highly placed spy. To guarantee Collins' anonymity, the Admiral never made any effort to meet the man, but demanded weekly reports, which were written directly by the staff sergeant and delivered to a handler in London who would, in turn, pass them to Canaris via diplomatic pouch.

Collins had previously heard of Operation Overlord, but Eisenhower's revelation about the makeup of the army groups and the massive numbers of troops involved was something new and extremely important. Admiral Canaris would be *very* pleased.

Chapter 13

By mission number five, which occurred only two weeks after Jack's indoctrination as a combat gunner, he was one of the veteran crewmen, and was expected to provide both instruction and encouragement to the newest members of the crew. Five of the men present during his first mission had rotated back to the states, having fulfilled their twenty mission obligation. One had been killed in action, and another was listed as missing. Private Saunders had been killed during a strafing run by German fighters on their base at Boreham. He was racing across the staging area to pick up two airmen who were working on a landing gear that had collapsed on one of the Fortresses, preventing it from taxiing to the maintenance hangar. Cannon shells hit his Jeep, causing an explosion that killed the airman instantly. Lieutenant Jeffers, copilot of Jack's original crew when Lieutenant Morgan had been promoted to captain and pilot of the aircraft, had volunteered for an additional flight in another Fortress after their copilot had been injured. His B-17 had been shot down near Bielefeld while on a mission to bomb a large munitions factory at Dresden. Observers from other aircraft in the formation reported the crippled Fortress flew under control to the ground, but the fate of the crew was unknown.

Captain Morgan and Lieutenant Holland both had more than enough missions to qualify for rotation home, as did Sergeant Freddy Lancaster, the other waist gunner Jack had met on his first mission. All three men, each for his own reasons, had chosen to stay on and help the war effort for at least a little longer. Morgan, Holland, Freddy Lancaster, and Jack comprised the veteran crew of "Hitler's Headache."

Jack had discovered that Lieutenant Holland was absolutely correct about the fear never going away. He had been just as terrified on the fifth mission as he had been on the first, but again, just as the lieutenant had said, after the first five minutes of combat, his body went on automatic pilot and the remainder of the grueling fight was just a blur. The private's skill with the Browning fifty caliber machine gun was becoming legendary throughout the bomb group. After his third mission, the former farm boy had shot down thirteen enemy aircraft confirmed, and probably four more. These numbers were unheard of in the Air Corps. Tail gunners usually accounted for the most confirmed kills, but even a good tail gunner usually completed his required rotation with less than twenty aircraft shot down.

B-17s flew in formation at about two hundred mph. German fighters had learned that the best angle of attack was from the front of the formation, because their speed added to that of the B-17s meant the gunners had to fire their moving, rotating guns at a target that was whisking by at over four hundred mph.

Guns on the German fighters were fixed, controlled only by the pilot as he aimed his aircraft at his enemy, so his task, combined with his speed and maneuverability gave him a distinctive edge over the larger, slower bombers. The fact that a waist gunner could hit so many aircraft traveling at such high speeds was phenomenal. As Jack's fame grew, it was not unusual for gunners from other squadrons, or even pilots and command officers, to seek him out between missions and ask for any advice or instruction he might have that could improve their own performance. Jack's answer, always delivered with an exaggerated country drawl, was usually, "Well, back home when I was huntin' ducks or doves or quail, I learned to judge their speed and lead 'em just enough to let 'em fly into the shot pattern." He would pause for a reflective moment then add, "'Course I was huntin' with an ol' single shot twelve gauge shotgun so I only got one chance at 'em. With that Browning fifty, I got so many shots I cain't hardly miss. Why, back home Daddy would whoop me if I used up that many shells and didn't bring down some ducks."

As a general rule, the enlisted men listened in awe, certain he was giving them good advice even if they didn't understand it. The officers, on the other hand, went away thinking he was either an idiot savant or just plain crazy. Either way, Jack enjoyed both the joke and the attention. Some airmen drank heavily to relieve the stress of their missions, some sulked, uncommunicative and hermit-like. Jack preferred to joke around, and found that it relieved not only his tension, but often that of the people around him as well.

Mission number six taught Jack and the rest of the crew a new dimension of fear as well as pride in their stamina and character when facing what appear to be insurmountable odds against them. Mission day weather was extremely bad, with minimal visibility and heavy rain. The flight was almost cancelled, but at the last minute the group meteorologist received a report that indicated clear skies over the target and improved weather at Boreham by the time the group returned.

"Hitler's Headache" broke through the clouds into a clear, cold sky at twenty thousand feet. They climbed to their preferred twenty five thousand foot cruising altitude and moved into cruise formation. Heavy cloud cover remained a few thousand feet below them for almost the entire flight and, along with a failed German radar station at Stuttgart, kept the group hidden from the usual fighter cover. Cloud cover dissipated less than twenty miles west of Dresden, their target for the fourth straight mission. What had been cloud cover was quickly replaced with the black smoke of anti-aircraft fire as the formation reached the outer edges of the city. Jack and the rest of the crew were reveling in the fact that they had just completed their first flight over Germany without the horror of attack by the Luftwaffe when their craft was hit very hard three times in succession by ack-ack explosions. Jack stood and gripped the cradle of his machine gun for stability as he looked out the window. Several feet of the port wing had been shredded by the cannon fire. It was primarily intact, but with giant holes that made it resemble a slice of Swiss cheese. The outboard engine was on fire and the aileron was completely missing.

Jack pressed his radio transmitter button. "Captain, you seeing this?" he asked. "The port wing looks almost like it did the first time we met. Can you get the fire out, sir?"

"Working on it," came the reply, then, "Jack, it looks like the aileron is gone. Can you check the inside control cable and make sure it still moves freely. The cable won't work for the other wing if the port side is fouled. If the cable moves freely, make sure it stays that way. If it's caught on something and won't move, cut it. It'll be sluggish, but I think I can control this thing with the rudder and one aileron if it works freely."

"Moving to the cable housing, Captain," Jack answered. He moved forward toward the overhead brackets that held the control cables, but was knocked off his feet by the explosion of a nearby shell.

"Everyone okay back there?" queried Lieutenant Holland from his perch in the turret, where he was observing the fire control system as the captain attempted to smother the flames from the disabled engine with the fire suppression canister that was housed in the engine nacelle and controlled by a switch on the instrument panel.

Freddie was helping Jack from the floor. The two men looked around at the rest of the crew, all newbies who were reacting as the veterans expected in the face of their first shelling. They looked to the rear and observed Private Neely worming his way backward out of the tail gun tunnel. Freddy thumbed his mike, "You okay, Neely?"

There was no answer until the man had backed completely out of the tunnel and sat up on the floor, crossing his legs into a Buddha posture. He gave them a thumbs up as his reply.

Jack thumbed his mike. "We're all okay back here. I'm still headed to the cable, but it looks loose from where I'm standing." He took the few steps to the cable housing and pulled on the one that ran to the port aileron. It moved freely. "Cable's okay, Cap."

"Thanks, Jack," came the reply. "I don't know how, but we're still in formation. There's no point in turning around in this flack, so I'm going to try to complete our bomb run with the rest of the group. Then we'll worry about limping home."

"Well, butter my butt and call me a biscuit, Cap," Jack answered. "You the man!" The radios hooted with laughter until the next ack-ack explosion hit hard enough to jar the fillings out of the crew's teeth.

Somehow Captain Morgan completed the bomb run and began his turn toward home. With only one aileron and the diminished lift and increased drag from the damaged wing, "Hitler's Headache" turned very slowly and inefficiently, taking several more miles to complete the maneuver than other aircraft in the formation. By the time he completed the turn, Morgan realized he was several miles north and far behind the rest of the group. They were all alone in a crippled airplane deep into enemy territory.

It was only then the newly assigned copilot said, "Oh, God! Oh, God, Captain. With all that happened back there...I haven't been watching the fuel. We're losing fuel, sir. Oh, God, I'm sorry. I should have been..."

"Calm down, Lieutenant," Morgan snapped. "Whether or not you were watching, we're losing fuel. There was nothing you could have done about it ten minutes ago even if you had noticed."

The conversation was heard throughout the ship, and there was complete silence for several minutes after the captain stopped speaking. Finally the crew heard him say, "Lieutenant Holland, can you calculate the rate of fuel drain? If we can figure out how long we can keep this thing in the air, maybe we can navigate to somewhere friendly...set 'Hitler's Headache' down in a safe place."

The crew's uplifted spirits after the captain's request were short lived. It only required a few minutes for the flight engineer to calculate that they could fly no more than an hour and only if the rate of fuel loss remained constant. If they remained on a heading for home, their fuel would take them to a point somewhere between Hannover and Dortmund. It was rough country, according to their topographical map, and still well within the borders of Germany, but it was land that was lightly populated. If the captain could set them down safely, there was a good chance they could sneak away from the crash site, somehow make it to the coast, and find a way back to England. The odds were long, but in their current situation, with a broken wing, a smoking engine, and a fuel leak, the crew preferred to think about making it home. The alternatives, death in a crash or at the hands of the Germans, or life in a prison camp, were too horrible to contemplate.

Captain Morgan was able to coax several more minutes of flight out of the crippled bird by leaning the fuel mixture to the max and adjusting their speed and their decent rate to provide the greatest possible distance. Luck was with them, and they landed roughly in a flat field about thirty miles northwest of Osnabruck. Cloud cover was still relatively heavy, and the Fortress didn't break out of the soup until the altimeter read six hundred feet. It made for a tense landing with very little time to find an adequate place to set down, but it did muffle the engine noise and prevent anyone except those in the immediate vicinity from seeing the aircraft. The damaged port wing crumpled as the bomber touched down, breaking the landing gear and causing the craft to spin to the left, but aside from bumps and bruises, the only damage to the crew was to the tail gunner, whose face was slammed against one of the steel ribs in the tail section, breaking his nose and one of his front teeth.

As soon as movement had stopped, Captain Morgan clicked on his microphone ordering everyone out of the plane just before he shut down all of the electronic systems. Minutes later the crew was assembled on a muddy field that looked very much like the one at Boreham before the Marsden runways had been constructed. They had landed next to a dilapidated barn, and could see what appeared to be a farm house about a hundred yards away. There were no lights in the house even though the late afternoon cloud cover made it quite dark. Morgan sent Jack and Freddy to reconnoiter the house while the rest of the men assembled in the barn. Several minutes later the recon team returned to report the house was empty and did not appear to have been lived in recently. Their luck was holding. Dreary weather and the low clouds had stilled any wind, and the men could hear no noise anywhere around them as darkness settled.

The house was northwest of the Fortress, and beyond the house was what appeared to be a heavily wooded area. Martin decided they would go to the house, which was more secure than the rickety barn, and assess their position with their maps and flashlights as well as search the house for any supplies or equipment that might be of use to them. Inside the men found little of value. There were a few scraps of cloth, which they used to cover the windows allowing careful use of their flashlights without allowing distant passersby to notice light coming from the abandoned house. There was a dirty and bloodied blouse from a German infantry uniform, but no food, cooking utensils, knives, or other tools that might be used as weapons. There was a table and two chairs, both of which had broken backs but serviceable seats. Captain

Morgan and Lieutenant Bronson, the new navigator, sat down and spread their topographical map and their flight charts out on the tabletop. Huddled over them with low light from one flashlight, they determined their location within a dozen miles or so. The shortest route to the sea, where they might be able to steal a boat and cross the channel to England, was due north, about ninety miles. There were no large cities or towns in the coastal area, and they had no idea of what they would find there. They also had no idea of the location of German bunkers or defensive units along the coast, or, for that matter, of German troop movements or encampments anywhere along the way. The entire route to the north would be within Germany, and they would be moving blind through enemy territory with no idea of what to expect when they reached their destination.

Another option was to travel due west from their position and attempt to reach Amsterdam. It was a longer journey, close to one hundred-fifty miles, but at least a portion of it would be in the Netherlands, which the officers thought might be safer. The Netherlands had tried to remain neutral when the war began, but were soon overrun by the German Army. Their government and monarchy had exiled themselves to England, and a very active resistance movement and clandestine system of transportation between the two countries was known to be maintained by an English/ Dutch paramilitary coalition. British and American flight officers were taught to memorize certain code words and phrases, which changed regularly, to use in conversation in case they were ever shot down and were able to make it into Dutch territory. Assuming their codes were current and they could make the journey undiscovered by German troops, Amsterdam appeared to be the most likely place for them to find a way back to England.

The decision having been made, the crew took inventory of their usable possessions. They had three flashlights, all with working batteries, and the maps currently being folded and put away. Each crewman had been issued an E-3A "Tape Lid" survival kit. The kit consisted of a rectangular plastic flask, the lid of which was held on with tape, ergo its name. When the lid was removed, the contents could be emptied and the flask used for storing water. Contents included purification tablets for the water, a small saw, foodstuff including bouillon powder, a chocolate bar, gum, matches, bandages, aspirin, dextrose tablets, and a compass. In addition to the survival kit, flight officers were issued a Colt .45 automatic pistol, thirty rounds of ammunition, and a six-inch knife and sheath.

They could fill their flasks with water from the canister on the Fortress, but would need more soon, as well as supplemental food, for traveling carefully and mainly at night, as would be necessary. Their journey could take two weeks or longer and at Captain Morgan's order, contents were emptied from the Tape Lid flasks and placed in pockets of their flight uniforms. Four crewmen were sent back to "Hitler's Headache" to fill the flasks. As soon as they returned, the crew headed west, moving as quickly as possible in the dark. They knew that dawn would bring discovery of their Fortress, and they needed to put many miles behind them.

An hour's travel brought them to a low knoll overlooking a gravel road that seemed to head in a northwesterly direction. Morgan decided they should waste some precious time by throwing a little 'film flam,' as he called it, at any Germans who might later trail the crew. While their desired direction was due west, the Captain directed them to turn south, following the ridge which generally paralleled the road. After half a mile, he directed them to work their way down the ridge, still moving in a southerly direction, until they intersected the road. Hopefully this ploy would fool the Germans into believing the group was taking the road southeast, when, in fact, they made an about face after reaching the center of the road and began to move quickly to the northwest. Unless the German troops were excellent trackers, they would never notice the boot marks on the packed gravel moving in the opposite direction.

Lieutenant Holland took point, moving a quarter mile forward of the rest of the crew, as they maintained a jogging pace for an hour. Holland moved at a faster pace, but stopped every few minutes to listen for any tell-tale sounds. Luck was still watching over the crew. Lieutenant Bronson estimated they had traveled about ten miles on the road before Captain Morgan decided it was time to leave the road and get back to their original heading—due west toward Amsterdam. They left the road at a brushy area that they hoped would hide their tracks. After only a few yards, the brush gave way to an open field that seemed, in the dark, to stretch forever in their desired direction. The men walked quickly across the soft ground, and by the time grey light was dawning in the east, they estimated they were twenty-two miles from the Fortress. It had been a good night's travel. Faint lights of a small village were visible north of their position, and the field appeared to continue endlessly to the west, so the group moved south to a copse of trees surrounding a narrow ditch, and spent a wet day hiding there. After listening to grumbles about the cold and damp, Jack stood wordlessly and moved along the ditch bank, keeping under cover of the trees. He disappeared through the foliage after fifty yards or so, but returned fifteen minutes later carrying dry kindling in his pockets and a few sticks of dry and aged wood. Striking a match from his Tape Lid kit, he started a small fire. With aged wood the flames would create very little smoke, and with careful placement of the small fire, leaves would dissipate the smoke, with little chance anyone would notice the encampment. The crew gratefully gathered around the fire a few at a time to warm their hands and faces. Later in the day, as hunger began gnawing at their bellies, he taught a couple of the crew how to make and set snares, hoping to catch some rabbits for lunch. They had no luck that first day, but kept the snares to try again at their next stop.

"How did you learn all of those woodsman skills, Jack?" Captain Morgan asked after watching the young private retrieve some dry grass from the pocket of his flight suit and use it to start a fire. "How do you learn to find dry wood and kindling when everything around us is soaking wet from days of rain?"

"Aw, Cap," Jack answered, embarrassed, "it's nothing anybody back home can't do. I guess I learned most of it from my Pop and my older brothers. We all grew up huntin' and fishin', sometimes so deep in the woods we couldn't make it back home at night, so we learned how to make a camp and a shelter, if it was raining, and find food and dry wood for a fire." He looked around. "'Course there weren't Germans looking for us, so we could usually shoot our food and build a bigger fire."

Morgan smiled and patted the airman on the back. "This one is just fine, Jack, and thanks from all of us. Now you should probably get some sleep if you can. Long night ahead of us."

The men slept in shifts and ate from their meager rations. There was little talk. They were scared and exhausted and far from home.

Chapter 14

Admiral Wilhelm Canaris was very interested, but not pleased. His hands shook slightly as he read and reread the report sent from Sergeant Michael Collins in England. This was a problem...a real problem. "Dieter, bring me a glass of Sherry," the head of the Abwer called out through the opened door to his secretary's office. He placed the report on his desk, face down, so the young man would not notice his tremor or see the content of the report. The Admiral then placed his hands on his lap and took a deep breath, exhaling slowly as he sat back in his chair. It was early for a drink, not yet three o'clock, but the Sherry would help calm his nerves so he could formulate a plan around this newly received information.

"Jawohl, Herr Admiral," answered the Hauptfeldwebel (staff sergeant) through the door. Minutes later he entered the room carrying a silver tray on which sat an elegant cut crystal glass filled with a dark mahogany liquid. He, too, was aware of the hour and, knowing his boss' drinking habits, asked, "Is everything all right, sir?"

"Yes, yes, I'm okay," Canaris answered impatiently. "Indicating the paper at the center his neatly organized desk, he explained, "Just some distressing news from one of our operatives. Nothing to worry yourself about."

He dismissed the sergeant, adding, "Please close the door on your way out and try to discourage anyone who wishes to bother me for the rest of today."

Admiral Canaris was an enigma...so much so that prosecutors at the Nuremburg trials after the war had ended could never decide if the man had been friend or foe to the Allies during the war. The Admiral's problem stemmed from the fact that he hated Hitler and his Nazis, but he loved Germany. Even though he headed a vast empire of intelligence gathering apparatus, he was an outsider in every respect within Hitler's inner circle, and reveled in that fact for several reasons.

Canaris was a somewhat frail and extremely timid man who of necessity put on an act of being a formidable leader any time he was required to meet with Hitler or Himmler, both of whom he despised with great intensity. He was very good at his job, and the Nazi hierarchy depended on him to keep them apprised of everything from enemy troop movements and concentrations to the personal mood of Churchill, Stalin, Eisenhower, and many others. The head of the Abwer fed them information constantly, most of which was accurate and verifiable. He had another side, however.

After witnessing the murder of Polish citizens and standing helpless and aghast as German troops herded two hundred Jews into a synagogue and set it on fire in 1939, Canaris swore to himself that he would work to break the back of the Nazi regime and bring his beloved Germany back to a government with sane leadership.

He made every possible effort from his position to save the lives of French, Russian, and particularly Jewish citizens who were victims of mass exterminations, primarily by Himmler's SS troops. On one occasion Canaris saved the lives of seven Jews by going directly to Himmler and complaining that he had arrested members in the Abwer staff.

His love/hate relationship with his country and its government gave him many sleepless nights and made him an indescribable mystery to all who met him. He rarely spoke, but was a great listener, a fact that made him the consummate superspy he was.

The Admiral was part of a vast conspiracy with other high ranking officers to kill Hitler. On the other hand, Hitler had heard rumors of the assassination plan, and engaged Canaris to track down the conspirators. He, along with his second in command, Hans Oster, provided the Allies with the details of Hitler's plan to invade England, while at the same time providing Hitler with accurate descriptions of Allied troop movements on the continent. The Admiral's life was a whirlwind of conflict and torn allegiance. When he read between the lines of this most recent report from Eisenhower's headquarters, it portended a massive invasion of France to push back the German Army. The report gave no indication of when or exactly where the invasion would occur, but Canaris was wily enough to assess the most likely points of ingress into France. An operation of this magnitude could crush Hitler's army and bring an end to the war.

How to use this information? Admiral Canaris wondered as he leaned back in his chair and sipped the Sherry. After setting down the glass, he tented his fingers on his chest and looked up at the ceiling. He would have to devise a plan.

Chapter 15

As night was waning in the eastern sky, Jack opened the door to the barn soundlessly and moved in to awaken the sleeping crew. He had the watch for the early morning hours. Having grown up in an area with many barns, all of which had steel hinges that would be rusty and squeaky after only a few years, he marveled at the handmade leather hinges, which were possibly decades old, but still held the door in a relatively straight position. The men had come upon this old barn, obviously unused for many years, about an hour before daybreak. They could have traveled a bit farther while cloaked in the darkness, but were tired and hungry, and needed food and rest. Moonlight had revealed a house in the distance as they had walked through the night, and Captain Morgan had sent two men to reconnoiter the structure. The dwelling was occupied, its residents probably sound asleep. The men discovered behind the house a brush arbor filled with produce, and stole as many potatoes and cabbages as they could carry.

When they reached the barn a few hours later, the spoils were distributed and the men feasted on raw potatoes and red cabbage. They would have preferred to make a soup, but had no pot in which to cook it. Their stomachs were empty, however, and they were very grateful for the raw produce. A meal, a few hours rest, and they would be ready for their sixth night of travel. So far the only enemy they had seen was an occasional Junkers transport or fighter flying high overhead.

After waking the men, Jack went back through the door to renew his watch until the group was ready to leave. As the door closed he was grabbed from behind by a large man who clamped his hand over Jack's mouth and dragged him away from the barn to what may have been a full platoon of German infantrymen. A cloth was shoved into his mouth, and his hands were roughly tied behind his back. A dozen men moved soundlessly across the soft earth and crashed through doors on either side of the barn, weapons at the ready. The barn was dark, but the crew had no doubt they had been invaded by German troops. All three officers pulled their weapons and fired in the general direction of the barn doors. The Germans returned fire, using the muzzle flashes as their aiming points. Bedlam ensued for the next several minutes before both sides proceeded with greater caution and the firing became sporadic. More Germans approached the barn and opened the doors wide as sunlight finally peeked over the horizon, allowing the combatants to finally see each other.

Two of the American crew's enlisted men had been killed in the melee, as had the navigator, Lieutenant Bronson. Captain Morgan had been hit, a through and through wound in the left side of his chest.

He was alive and conscious, but in great pain. Only one German was killed, but six others had been wounded, two seriously. The infantry platoon had a medic within its numbers, and the man proved to be quite skilled as he treated the wounds of both his countrymen and Captain Morgan. The American officer was treated surprisingly gently as the men were herded across the field to an awaiting truck. He was placed on a litter and lifted into an ambulance along with two of the German wounded. The rest of the men were ordered at gunpoint into the back of an Opel Blitz, Germany's answer to the venerable "deuce and a half" used by Allied troops throughout the war.

Two Germans armed with machine pistols rode in the back of the truck with the crewmen. None of the troops had given any indication that they spoke English.

Freddy looked at Jack with understandable fear in his eyes. "Looks like we may have made our last flight," he said glumly. "It's prison camp or firing squad from here." The rookie crew members flinched and looked at each other in alarm.

"Sei ruhig!" commanded one of the guards, pointing his machine pistol menacingly at Freddie. There was no doubt what the man was saying. "Shut up!"

The men were transported in the middle truck of a seven vehicle convoy. The ambulance carrying Captain Morgan was just in front of them, and the other trucks, as best the crew could tell in the dark, carried at least a platoon of infantrymen. They rode in silence for two hours, headed in a westerly direction. About nine o'clock a.m., the lead truck in the convoy exploded in a ball of intense flames. Rifle and machine gun fire erupted from the woods on both sides of the road. The German troops returned fire in the general direction of the attack, but had no direct targets.

The two guards in the crew's truck stood and pointed their machine guns at the frightened men. "Keine Bewegung!" (don't move), shouted one of them, a pimply faced soldier no more that eighteen years old. Their attention was momentarily diverted by another explosion, this one at the rear of the convoy. They turned to see another truck full of troopers engulfed in flames. Heavy machine gun fire raked the other trucks, all except the middle one and the ambulance. After a few minutes there was screaming from both sides of the road as the attackers ran toward what remained of the convoy. Sporadic fire coming from one of the trucks was quickly quelled by one of the assault force as he raked the vehicle with fire from a Thompson submachine gun. A dozen of the force approached the center truck and pointed their rifles toward the two guards until the two young men threw their weapons out of the truck and held up their hands in surrender. Most of the platoon was dead, but seven other prisoners were picked up among the rubble of trucks and cargo. Along with the two guards of the Fortress crew, the Germans were roughly pushed into the woods to some unknown fate.

A tough looking man in civilian clothes with a Thompson slung over his shoulder climbed into the truck. In halting English he asked, "American flyers?" The crew nodded in unison. Lieutenant Holland arose and said, "Yes, sir, we're Americans. And you?"

The man smiled broadly, revealing two missing front teeth. "We are Dutch resistance! We fight the Bosch! We fight good!" He explained further. "Our spies heard of you and how the Germans would capture you. We decided," he slapped his chest with his hand, "we would capture you back!"

Holland held out his hand. "Thank you, thank you, sir, for coming to our aid."

The man ignored the lieutenant's hand, saying, "Now we go. More Bosch come soon." He climbed out of the truck, followed by Holland, Jack, and the rest of the crew. The men of the Dutch resistance surrounded them with smiles, pats on the back, and many comments of which the men had no idea of what was said. They moved through the woods for about an hour, finally emerging onto a dirt track on which sat three captured German trucks. The crew happily boarded the open bed truck and found Captain Morgan lying on the floor alive and awake. He grimaced as the vehicle jerked to a start, then closed his eyes and smiled as his crew began the first leg of their journey home.

Chapter 16

Ike was in an uncharacteristically foul mood. Months before, General Patton had slapped a private who was in a field hospital, having been diagnosed with exhaustion. Patton had called him a coward and reportedly reached for his holstered revolver to shoot the man if he didn't shape up and rejoin his combat unit. The incident had been witnessed by several people in the hospital, but had gone unnoticed by the media until recently. Suddenly, the story was being broadcast around the world. Beetle Smith was livid, and had called General Eisenhower to demand Patton be immediately fired. Those sentiments had been echoed by most other allied field commanders, who were tired of the arrogant Patton's tirades. Ike was resisting the pressure, for he knew Patton was his most talented field commander, and was very likely the man on whose shoulders victory in Europe would ultimately rest. His resolve did not lessen the pressure to remove Patton, however, leaving him ill-tempered and feeling on the verge of a tension headache.

To make matters worse, new intelligence of a completely different, but no less critical nature, had been waiting for him as he reached headquarters this morning. It was information that required immediate action, so the commanding general forced himself to remove all thoughts of the Patton problem from his mind, and concentrate on this perilous issue first.

General Eisenhower had moved Lieutenant Colonel Martin into a large office adjacent to his own. There was no door between them, only an elaborate arched opening, a fact which allowed the younger officer to hear every conversation that occurred in the commander's office. Martin wasn't certain he wanted that kind of responsibility, but he was, after all the Chief of Staff. As such, he was privy to all that transpired at Supreme Allied Headquarters. The office was large, and included more than enough room for Charlie to have a work space as well. In the several weeks he had been at SHAEF, Eisenhower had come to like the young sergeant, appeared to trust him implicitly, and recognized the shrewdness of the young man's character and his value as Colonel Martin's aide. Ike had heard the assessment that his chief of staff and Charlie were joined at the hip, and he believed that was true on several levels.

"Colonel Martin, can you come in immediately," Eisenhower growled, perhaps a little more gruffly than he would have preferred. "And bring Charlie with you."

Martin didn't answer, but he and Charlie arose from their own desks and walked quickly to the commander's elaborately carved cherry wood desk. There were only two items on the highly polished desktop, a telephone placed at one corner and a folder marked TOP SECRET placed directly in the center. The general picked up the folder as the two men approached and said, "This just arrived by courier. The information is disturbing and very problematic." He arose and began to walk toward the main door to his office, still carrying the top secret folder. "Come with me," he ordered as he opened the door and entered the vast lobby. Charlie looked questioningly at his Colonel, but followed a few paces behind as the two officers exited the room and walked briskly across the wide lobby to the building's entrance.

At the massive double door, Ike turned to the two men and said very softly, "You know I have standing orders that no top secret papers are to leave this building at any time. I'm making an exception to those orders." He opened the door and walked out into a surprisingly bright and warm English fall afternoon. The three men walked in silence for several minutes before entering a small park lined with trees and filled with several statues of World War I heroes. They entered a small courtyard surrounded by a low limestone block wall and General Eisenhower sat down on one of several stone benches. He motioned for the colonel and sergeant to sit as well, saying, "Please sit, gentlemen, we need to talk."

He opened the folder and passed a single sheet of paper to Martin. "I have a working relationship with the head of Hitler's intelligence organization, the Abwer." He said flatly, then paused to allow the import of the statement to soak in.

"Sir, did you say the *head* of the Abwer...as in Admiral Canaris?" Martin asked with incredulity in his tone.

Ike nodded and answered grimly, "Admiral Wilhelm Canaris, World War I submariner, decorated military hero, master spy, chief of all intelligence operations for the Reich...and part-time double agent working for the Allies...for me."

Martin started to say something, but the General stopped him by raising his hand. "It's incredible, I know. Canaris is a very gifted and highly unusual man who dearly loves his country, but has a deep hatred for all the evil Hitler, Himmler, and the Nazi regime have brought to Germany. He knows Germany must lose the war in order for Hitler and his cronies to be driven from power and, hopefully, punished, but he wants Germany and her people to survive as unscathed as possible when the Nazis are defeated. He is orchestrating a masterful juggling act which, even though technically treason against his government, might be the most patriotic act I have ever encountered."

Ike held up the folder. "This information is from Canaris. He knows about Operation Overlord...very specific things such as the army group organization and the number of troops involved. As might be expected, he sees it as an opportunity to crush the Reich. He has asked me to provide him with specific details of the operation so he can offer suggestions and put in place a series of intelligence reports that will confuse and mislead Hitler as to the nature of the impending invasion."

Charlie blurted, "Begging your pardon, sir, but if the Germans know about Operation Overlord, doesn't that mean..."

Eisenhower cut him off, "We have a spy at SHAEF." He looked at Charlie. "Excellent deduction, Sergeant. We have an ally in Canaris, but we have a spy in our midst. There are no more than twenty people at headquarters who know the details we've worked out so far. I have to assume, could not believe otherwise, that Generals Smith, Marshall, Bradley, Air Marshall Tedder, and Field Marshall Montgomery, are all patriots. They are all architects of parts of the plan, and all has been done in secret, without input from or knowledge by even their most trusted staff. We have played this very close to the vest." He looked disgusted for a moment before saying, "Of course, there are the politicians. I certainly trust Churchill and President Roosevelt, but both have political staffs and advisors, and I have little control over what they say to whom...but I really believe the leak is coming from within our own headquarters. That's why we're having this discussion here," he motioned around, "instead of in my office."

Martin spoke tentatively, "Sir, regarding your office...if I was a spy, I would want to be as close to the top as possible. As you said, the other generals and politicians may have knowledge of much of the invasion plan, but *you,* sir, are the collection point. At any given moment, you may be the only one who has the complete plan in its latest form. I hate to say it, General, but your most likely spies are myself, Charlie, and the four enlisted men in the office opposite ours."

Eisenhower looked at the ground. "That was my assessment as well, Jerry," he said sadly, using the lieutenant colonels nickname, as he often did when they were alone. "Based on your history...yours, too, Charlie, the fact that you came straight here from the States, and my assessment of your character in the few months we have worked together, I don't think either of you has been corrupted by the Nazis. You're not my spies," he concluded with his trademark smile. The smile evaporated as he said, "That leaves Staff Sergeant Collins and the other three assistants, all of whom take care of my daily correspondence, help to arrange my schedule, and, of course, are privy to most of what goes on in my office, as I seldom close the door to their adjoining office. Corporal Allen and Sergeant Varrick are Americans, Staff Sergeant Collins and Sergeant Long are British. I hate to think of any of them as traitors, but I admit they are the most likely culprits."

Ike looked at Charlie. "Charlie, you're very good at finding out personal information about people, and you probably already have a partial dossier on those four men." He smiled once more and added, "You may even have a dossier on *me!*" He watched as the young man blushed, then said, "I want you to use your talents and find out as much as you can about those men. Also, I'll give you a list of everyone at SHAEF who has a working knowledge of the major parts of Operation Overlord, and I will be grateful if you will look into them as well."

The sergeant's face was still red as he answered, "Yes, sir, I can do that. And sir," he added timidly, "It's only a very small file I have on you."

The Supreme Allied Commander laughed loudly, making Charlie's face turn an even deeper shade of crimson. He turned to Colonel Martin and said, "Jerry, I have a different job for you. When we return to SHAEF, I will give you the complete file I have on Operation Overlord. It is not the final plan, of course, but I want you to familiarize yourself with all aspects of it. Any ideas you might have for the operation itself, and any assessment of how we might use Canaris, I want to know as quickly as possible. Never bring up the subject in my office, of course. I will find a better place for us to talk," he looked at Charlie, "until the spy problem is solved."

He was silent for several minutes, watching a group of young children kicking a ball back and forth. Finally he stood, saying, "I think that is enough for now. Thank you, gentlemen. I know I can depend on you."

Chapter 17

Three months and sixteen missions later, Jack was considering going home. He had a total of twenty-two bombing missions, two over the number that gave him the right to rotate back to the States. The bombing runs after the crash and escape with the aid of the Dutch resistance had been harrowing, of course, but that was the nature of the business. He had completed his missions with no injuries, but could tell the stress of almost constant combat was wearing on him. It distressed the young man to look in the mirror at the wrinkles on his brow and the few grey hairs that were beginning to show on top of his head. He was only twenty years old, but was beginning to look as old as some of the squadron's pilots, many of whom were almost thirty. The private's prowess as waist gunner had made him famous throughout the bomb groups, and he was very proud of the fact that he had personally shot down at least sixty four enemy aircraft, and possibly a couple dozen more.

Two weeks after their escape from Germany, the remaining crew of 'Hitler's Headache' had been split up to fill vacancies in the crew positions of three other B-17s. Jack, Freddie, and Lieutenant Holland had all been assigned to a Flying Fortress named 'Mickey's Marauders.' The aircraft sported a caricature of Walt

Disney's Mickey Mouse as nose art, and had flown forty seven precision bombing missions since its activation. Four of the crewmen were veterans of eighteen of those missions at the time the three replacements joined their number. They were ecstatic to discover that Jack was joining them as a waist gunner and, in a brief and secret meeting, decided to rename their Fortress in his honor. Jack was shocked and embarrassed on the morning of his first mission in the new B-17 to find the nose art had been changed to a painting of a knight in medieval armor jousting with a fifty Caliber machine gun. The name under the painting was 'Sir Jack.'

Sometimes at night the airman would wake up thinking about the enemy pilots, not the aircraft. Did they have families who would miss them? Did they have dreams for after the war? Were they just young men like himself, who didn't really understand all the reasons they were fighting, but were simply doing the job which they had been taught to do?

Jack had even spoken with one of the regimental chaplains about his thoughts and regrets. The chaplain had patted his arm and suggested, "Your military record of achievement shows you're a good soldier. Your regrets about killing the enemy show that you are also a good man. Maybe it's time you went home. This war will end one day, and I have no doubt you will find something positive to do with your life...something that will be pleasing in the eyes of God."

It was time to go home, Jack decided. He went to the squadron commander's office and filled out the proper request forms. He was aware that processing out sometimes took several weeks, and had known of a few crewmen who had been killed on missions while waiting for their transfer orders. It was the time bomber crews hated and feared the most.

Less than two weeks later, only a few days before Christmas, Jack was called to the squadron commander's office. Major Isaacson rose from behind his desk as the sergeant entered his office and said, "Jack, we're sorry to be losing you. You've done a great job in more ways than you know."

"Sir?" the young man questioned.

The major laughed. "Your gunnery record is unmatched anywhere in the Air Corps. It has made you quite the celebrity."

Jack blushed, and said, "Well, sir, I was just doing what I was taught. I guess I'm a good shot, but there are a lot of good gunners out there. I've even helped a few of them learn how to shoot better."

"I'm aware of that," answered the commander. "What you probably don't know is that your personal celebrity has brought quite a bit of attention to this bomb group over the last few months. We've actually been able to get parts, ordinance, even replacement aircraft and crews much faster than other groups just because the brass above us knows of you and what you've done. It makes them proud, and they want to do everything they can for us."

Jack was silent for a moment, finally saying, "Wow, sir. I didn't know any of that. Are you saying it would be better if I stay?"

"No, Sergeant," Isaacson said with a chuckle. "Naturally we would be happy if any man of your talents stayed with us, but you have done enough here. Actually, the Air Corps has another assignment for you stateside. I have orders for your transfer to Kingman Army Airfield in Arizona. You are to be an instructor at the aviation gunnery school. I can't think of a man better suited for the job." He curled his lip in a disgusted expression. "I was there once, just before the war. Kingman is in the desert in the middle of nowhere. Nothing but rattlesnakes for a hundred miles in any direction. But," his face brightened, "it's a damn site better that being shot at every day while you're five miles above Germany." The officer surprised Jack by extending his hand. "Good luck, soldier...and thank you for your exceptional service to your country."

Jack was thoroughly embarrassed, but thrilled to be going home. He stammered, "Yes, sir...thank you, sir," as he turned to leave the office.

"Oh, Jack," the Major said as an afterthought, "unless something changes, you're not scheduled to leave until after Christmas. Headquarters says there will be no flights back to the States until December 27. I guess you'll have to put up with our mess hall's version of Christmas dinner." He smiled warmly and concluded, "Dismissed, Sergeant."

Chapter 18

Thanksgiving Day 1943 found most of the staff at SHAEF hard at work at their desks or on assignment at various locations across Europe. Complete transfer of command from Allied Forces Headquarters in Algeria to the SHAEF headquarters in London had been accomplished less than two months earlier. The closing down of AFHQ had freed up General Eisenhower and many of his senior staff members from constant travel between the headquarters, and given them time to work on projects more directly related to the war effort. A sumptuous Thanksgiving dinner was planned for the entire staff and several guests later in the day, but for the moment work continued as usual.

Charlie had been absent all morning, not an unusual event since he had been given the task of ferreting out the spy in SHAEF several weeks before. Colonel Martin was reaching for his telephone when Charlie rushed breathlessly into the room. He slowed his pace, glanced into Ike's office to find the commander was not in, and walked directly to Martin's desk.

He pulled up a chair next to the officer, leaned over very close, and whispered, "It's Collins, sir." Glancing once more into Eisenhower's office, or, more precisely, through the door to Sergeant Collins' desk to see if the man was looking at them, he continued, "Staff

Sergeant Collins is the spy. There's no doubt. We need to talk somewhere else, sir."

Martin glanced through the doors toward Sergeant Collins, who appeared not to have noticed the men's conversation. He quickly understood and picked up the subterfuge by saying loudly, "That's right, Charlie. Great idea. We need to tell the quartermaster right now." He stood, indicating for Charlie to do so as well. As the men walked briskly from the office, they noticed Sergeant Collins watching them, attracted, no doubt by the outburst from Colonel Martin.

Charlie nodded a greeting in his direction and hurried after the colonel. A cold rain was falling outside, and the two men had no desire to travel to the park where they often talked with Ike. Directly across the street from SHAEF, the street having recently been renamed Shaef Way, was an abandoned hotel building that was being renovated for additional military offices.

Since it was a holiday, albeit an American one, even the British construction crews had taken the day off, leaving the building empty. Martin and Charlie walked through the unlocked door and found a large room that had once been the reception area. There was a large stone fireplace on one side, and an old Victorian sofa and several plush chairs, all worn and threadbare, arranged around the hearth. The building was cold, but much preferable to the rain outside, so the two men sat down.

Charlie was flush with excitement. "I've found the spy, sir," he said with breathless enthusiasm. Speaking rapidly, he continued, "I checked out just about everyone, just to be sure, but I found out some things early on that made me suspect Collins. It took several weeks to put it all together because I had to be careful to hide my interest, but I finally figured it all out." The Sergeant was speaking so quickly that Martin was having some difficulty understanding all he said.

"Calm down, Charlie," the officer finally said, leaning over to put a hand on the young man's shoulder. "Slow down, speak calmly, and tell it from the beginning."

Charlie took a deep breath and exhaled slowly. "Staff Sergeant Collins is Irish, not British. I always thought that was kind of like being from Colorado instead of Michigan, but it's not. Things like that are a lot different over here." He watched Martin nod his head in agreement, and continued, "Anyway, there was an Irish revolution back around 1920, when Sergeant Collins was just a little boy. The war was between some of the Irish who wanted independence, and the British who ruled them...kind of like our American Revolution, I guess. One of the Irish leaders was named Michael Collins, just like the staff sergeant. He was a distant relative of the sergeant's and his family was in favor of the revolution, so his parents named him after the leader they admired so much." He stopped for a moment, then asked, "Am I still talking too fast, sir. Am I doing okay?"

"You're doing great, Charlie," answered the lieutenant colonel. "Sergeant Collins was named after an Irish revolution leader who was related to his family. Go on."

Charlie took another big breath. "Later, the sergeant's mom, dad, and older sister were killed when the British Army bombed their village. Collins was adopted by an uncle who fought with the Irish and hated the British. From the time he was a little boy, the sergeant has been taught to hate the British. He moved to London and joined the Army just so he might have a chance some day to sabotage the Army or the British government." He stopped for a moment before saying, "I couldn't find any proof that he is a German spy, sir, but it *has* to be him! It just *has* to be! All the pieces fit. What would be the odds of someone else hating us so much that they..." he let the thought trail off, and stopped, looking exhausted.

"Charlie, how did you..." Martin began, but then thought better of asking the question. "No, never mind. I probably don't even want to know." He looked thoughtful for a long moment before saying, "You must be right, but we need some kind of proof." Both men were silent for an extended period.

Finally, Charlie said, "Colonel, if I understand it right, Collins takes information he hears from General Eisenhower's office and somehow gets it to this Admiral Canaris in Germany. If it's important enough, the Admiral passes some of the information back to General Eisenhower, but doesn't tell him it came from Collins. Is that about right, sir?"

Martin's nod prompted Charlie to continue, "Could you and the General figure out something Collins could steal, something that sounds important, but really isn't the truth at all, and wait to see if the General hears anything back from this Canaris fellow that would confirm Collins was the one passing the information?"

Martin stared at the elaborate chandelier for a few moments, finally saying, "Very good, Charlie. I'm certainly glad you're on *our* side. That is really a great idea. Come on," he said, standing. "We need to find Ike."

Eisenhower was absent for the remainder of the day, but returned in the evening for the Thanksgiving feast. He brought to the dinner as guests Prime Minister Winston Churchill and several members of the British royalty, including two dukes, a baronet, and their families. With such elegant and important guests at the head table, there was no opportunity for Lieutenant Colonel Martin to gain even a brief audience with the general. Charlie's information would have to wait until the next day.

As soon as Ike arrived at his desk on Friday morning, Martin approached and handed him a single sheet of paper. He noticed that Staff Sergeant Collins was watching him as he said, "Good morning, General. Here are those statistics you asked me to find on shipping from the ports in Scotland."

Collins looked away, uninterested, as Eisenhower first looked questioningly at the lieutenant colonel, then looked at the paper handed him. It said simply, "Charlie found the spy. We need to talk whenever convenient for you."

"Thank you, Colonel," Eisenhower said while still looking at the paper. He handed it back to Martin and asked, "Would you keep this in your file along with the other shipping information you're compiling. And thank Admiral Winslow for helping us on this project." His lips curled in a slight smile. The general obviously enjoyed a little cloak-and-dagger thrown into his day. "By the way, Colonel, I have a meeting scheduled with Beetle Smith at his Kensington office at 1300 hours today. Could you accompany me?"

"Certainly, sir," answered Martin, understanding that the meeting time was set.

"And bring Charlie along." He laughed. "I really like that boy...he's a sharp one for such a young kid, and only went to the ninth grade, I understand." Ike looked thoughtful for a moment. "Given a little education, I suspect he could be just about anything. We may have to look into that someday...after the war is over, of course." He looked directly at Martin. "One o'clock, then?"

"Yes, sir." Martin answered, then returned to his desk.

Chapter 19

At 1300 hours sharp, Eisenhower arose from his desk and looked through the door to Staff Sergeant Collins. "Sergeant Collins," he said, "I'll likely be out for the remainder of the day. If I'm needed, contact General Smith. You know the drill. Thank you, Staff Sergeant." Ike was informal with many of his enlisted staff, but he knew the British did not think well of such familiarity, and preferred to be addressed by their rank, so the general obligingly did so.

He glanced through the arch into Lieutenant Colonel Martin's office, and saw the man stand and pick up what appeared to be a heavy leather briefcase. Charlie was clearing some paperwork from the top of his nearby desk, but quickly arose and followed the two officers out the door. A Rolls Royce staff car was awaiting them just outside.

The driver, a British Army corporal, held open the back door for all three of the men. The roomy cabin contained two bench seats that faced each other. Eisenhower slid into one of the seats, while Colonel Martin and Charlie took the other. There was a thick glass between them and the driver, but the general didn't wish to discuss important matters just in case the driver could hear them. Instead, they made small talk for the hour long drive. Ike was very interested when he learned Charlie had played semi-pro baseball before the war. They discussed what that was like, and various aspects of professional baseball, now that many of the stars had been drafted into the armed services. The general was a gifted conversationalist, and the drive went quickly.

They arrived at the Port of London, and the limousine finally stopped at a ramp leading up to a decrepit looking old warship. Ike climbed from the car and stood on the dock looking fondly at the ancient ship. When Martin and Charlie joined him, he said, "She doesn't look like much now, but this is the HMS Achilles, a Warrior-class armored cruiser with a distinguished record from World War I." He started up the ramp onto the ship and called back, "Come aboard. I'll show you something special."

Intrigued, Martin and Charlie hurried up the gangway to catch up with the general. As they reached him and walked across an unkempt wooden deck littered with long unused naval detritus, Eisenhower explained, "Prime Minister Churchill was First Lord of the Admiralty during the early years of World War I. For some reason he never explained to me, he had a special love for this ship. After the war ended, a British business consortium that included Churchill's family bought the decommissioned cruiser with a thought toward turning it into a small passenger ship. It never happened, but Churchill came here often after the war, and finally decided to convert part of the old girl as a 'home away from home,' so to speak. His idea of a getaway place is a little more elaborate than you might expect.

The men had reached a heavy bulkhead, rusted and looking as if it had not been opened in decades. Eisenhower reached for the large latch, which turned easily in his hand. The door swung silently on the apparently rusted hinges, surprising his companions. The three men descended steel stairs bordered by grey walls and walked down a well-lighted but narrow hallway, their footsteps echoing on the metal flooring. Finally they reached a weathered and old wooden door. General Eisenhower grasped the knob and pushed the door open, then stood back and motioned for the other two men to enter. He smiled as he heard both of them take a sharp breath as they entered the room.

The brightly lighted room was as large as a hotel lobby, and even better appointed. Walls were of highly polished mahogany, with elaborately carved crown molding where they met the ceiling. A long bar, also made of mahogany, stretched along one wall, and a billiard table was located on the other side. Several plush chairs were strategically located around the room, along with small tables which might accommodate card games or provide places to work. Several Persian carpets were artfully spaced over the hardwood flooring. The room was both formal and relaxing, possibly the perfect place for gentry and royalty to meet, work, or relax.

Eisenhower showed his two guests through another door into a lavish dining room that would accommodate twenty people around an ancient looking table, the top of which, Ike explained, had been constructed of decking taken from the HMS Beagle, the ship, commanded by Robert FitzRoy, on which Charles Darwin had made his famous voyage.

They returned to the main room, where Ike showed them to seats around a small table on which they could arrange their papers. Before they began, he told them a little more about the renovation of the Achilles. "There are six well appointed bedrooms on the ship, a modern kitchen, and, topside, a very nice sun deck where dignitaries can bask in the sun while being protected from casual onlookers. In other words," he said brightly while motioning around, "this is a great place to hide out for a day or a month. Churchill has been kind enough to offer the Achilles to me for use when I need to meet privately and securely with others, or when I just feel the need to get away myself."

He looked around with reverence at the room, finally saying, "According to Mr. Churchill, the Achilles was involved in nine different naval battles in World War I. She was nearly sunk near Gibraltar, but somehow managed to limp back to England with the help of an American destroyer that detached itself from a convoy to act as escort for the old girl. Later in the war, and possibly as retribution against the Germans, her captain rammed a U-boat in the north sea during a battle that included at least twenty Allied and German ships."

"Now, Charlie," the Supreme Commander said, suddenly changing the subject while looking intently at the young sergeant, "tell me about the spy, and what you think we should do about him."

Charlie repeated the information he had given to Lieutenant Colonel Martin, adding some additional facts that helped to confirm his suspicions. In speaking with several of the British enlisted men at SHAEF, he had discovered that Staff Sergeant Collins was uniformly disliked. He seemed not to get along with any of the British troops and was always talking about the heroes of the Irish revolution. Often his complaints about British mistreatment of the Irish expanded to include veiled threats against some of the oldest of the military brass and Members of Parliament who were around during the Irish war. Charlie never offered his suspicions of Collins' association with the Germans to any of the British staffers, but he got the distinct impression through his conversations that none of them would be surprised to learn the staff sergeant was an enemy spy.

Ike listened without interruption until Sergeant Bradley had finished. After taking a moment to mentally collate the facts he had been given, the general asked, "What do you think we should do with him? I certainly don't doubt the veracity of your story, and I agree with your conclusions, but there's no proof included in your report...only extreme suspicion. We must have some kind of definitive, irrefutable proof before accusing this man of treason." He offered a wry smile before continuing, "The British are our Allies, of course, but they still don't trust us completely. We're still just colonials in their eyes, I guess. Charging a Brit with such a crime, particularly without proof, will doubtless cause problems up the chain of command." He looked at Martin and asked "Don't you agree, Jerry?"

Martin answered quickly, "Yes, sir, I agree completely. Charlie and I have discussed those exact concerns...except for the Brits thinking of us as colonials. I didn't know that, sir. You mean they haven't gotten over the Revolutionary War yet?"

"Apparently not," Ike answered with a chuckle.

"Charlie came up with an idea of how to get proof, General," Martin stated.

Eisenhower turned to the sergeant with raised eyebrows. "Let's hear it, Sergeant," he said, eyes twinkling. "You never cease to amaze me, Charlie. Bright, hard working, and devious enough to be a confidence man...and only a ninth grade formal education, is that right?"

"Eighth grade, sir," Charlie answered with a perplexed look, "and I'm not so sure how formal it was. It was just a country school."

Eisenhower bellowed laughter. When he finally stopped, he said, "Let's hear this idea of yours, soldier."

Charlie explained his rather simple idea of making certain Staff Sergeant Collins received some kind of information that was all untrue, but sounded feasible and was of great enough importance that Collins would pass it along to Admiral Canaris. Hopefully, if it was the right kind of information, the Admiral would communicate to General Eisenhower that he knew of the information.

"If that happens, sir, then there won't be any doubt that Sergeant Collins is the spy." Charlie stopped for a moment as Eisenhower watched him intently. Finally he continued, "Sir, It's just a very general plan. I really didn't know what kind of information would be important enough to make Admiral Canaris contact you through his spy channels, but Colonel Martin came up with something that sounds good to me."

Ike turned to Martin. "You two make a good tag team. I suppose you will now tell me the details of the devious plan you two have hatched." He smiled again. "I'm certainly glad that both of you are working for the Allies."

Martin opened his case, extracted several papers, and laid out a large detailed map of the east coast of England, the English Channel, and the entire west coast of France. "

"Sir, I have studied the plans you have to date for Operation Overlord. The operation calls for a large force to land in a hundred fifty mile long front between Cherbourg and Le Havre." He indicated the area on the map. "I understand the specific landing points will represent a somewhat smaller area once details of fortifications and topography are calculated, but this is the general area of the invasion." He looked up at the general, who nodded his agreement. "I also understand from the reports that the Germans have heavy fixed fortifications...pill boxes, gun emplacements, and so on, along the Channel coast of France and Belgium." His fingers pointed a broad sweep across the map.

"The Germans are certain an invasion is coming, but they're unsure of the specific landing point, or points, and certainly don't have enough manpower to mount a heavy defense of this entire coastline."

"Correct on all counts, Colonel," Ike confirmed. "Go on."

"At some point, they'll be forced to make a guess based on their most current information, and move the large bulk of their defensive force to that likely point of ingress. My suggestion, sir, is that we devise an elaborate deception, a ruse, if you will, that will convince the German high command that the invasion will come at some point on the coast other than where we're actually planning, forcing them to move much of their force away from the face of the actual landings."

Eisenhower was impressed. "We've touched on this kind of idea in some of the more recent joint planning sessions, but no one has formulated an actual plan. What's your suggestion?"

"Based on your intelligence reports, General, many of the German commanders believe the attack will come at Calais." He pointed to a spot on the map far to the north of the planned invasion. "It makes great sense. Dover to Calais is by far the shortest route across the Channel. The invasion force could be there quickly and could easily attack a line from Calais up to Dunkerque and push inland over relatively flat ground to Lille. If I was planning to defend against an invasion from England, that's exactly where I would put my force. But there's a second element, sir."

Eisenhower said nothing, but raised his eyebrows in question.

"The Germans are convinced that General Patton will spearhead the invasion. I'm convinced of that, too. Specific commanders for the various armies and groups are not included in this plan, sir," he pointed to the thick sheaf of papers he placed on the table, "but Patton makes sense. He is the..."

"Patton!" Ike growled, his entire demeanor suddenly changing from complete interest in the presentation to absolute disgust at the mention of his most aggressive commander. "It's not enough that I have to put up with the constant complaints and egotistical whining of Field Marshall Montgomery; I must also put up with Patton." He glared at the lieutenant colonel.

Finally his internal rage subsided, and he said softly, "Please accept my apology, Colonel. You're correct. George Patton is without doubt the most aggressive commander, the best tactical planner, and the purest warrior on either side of this war. Pardon me for being so disparaging of the great man, but he is also a pompous, self-centered jerk whose mouth is often working far ahead of his brain and completely contrary to the desires of his superiors, his president, and the Allies in general. He has managed to anger the French, the Russians, most of the commanders at SHAEF, and the Brits by shooting off his mouth in the most undiplomatic of ways. Most recently he has stirred up a hornet's nest by slapping a tired and frightened soldier in front of a hundred witnesses. He's been considered to command the entire invasion force, but at this point I don't think any of his superiors, particularly the British, would stand for that."

He stopped for a moment and looked directly into the lieutenant colonel's eyes. "Quite frankly, Jerry, I'm thinking of sending him back to the States just to get him out of our hair. Possibly make him Commander of the United States Military Academy. It would be quite embarrassing for him, and he doesn't really deserve that, but I need to put him in his place."

The Supreme Commander suddenly looked tired. "I'm going to mobilize 3rd Army soon, and put it to use after the invasion. I may put Patton in command, but it will be good for him to cool his heels for a while...learn a little diplomacy, some respect." He straightened. "So no, Colonel, General Patton will *not* lead the invasion force."

Profound silence filled the room for several minutes. The three men listened to the soulful moan of a distant steamship whistle as it made its way up the Thames.

Finally Lieutenant Colonel Martin spoke. "Sir, I'm sorry. I didn't know any of that. I knew General Patton had always been, uh, controversial, but I didn't know it was so serious." He paused briefly before venturing, "Sir, I may have an idea how to use General Patton to our advantage, and at the same time force him to 'cool his heels,' as you put it."

General Eisenhower was interested. He held up an index finger and said, "One minute." Looking at Charlie, he said, "Charlie, there's a very excellent bottle of Chartron la Fleur chilling in the refrigerator behind the bar." He indicated the near end of the mahogany bar. "Would you mind uncorking it and bring us three glasses?"

"Yes, sir," the Sergeant answered and headed toward the bar. He found the refrigerator which, luckily, contained only one bottle. He fumbled with it for several minutes, prompting Eisenhower to ask, "Is there a problem, Charlie?"

"I'm sorry, sir," Charlie said, "but I'm just a farm boy. I don't have any idea how to open this."

Ike nodded and smiled as he arose to move to the bar. "That's okay, Charlie. I understand. One of these days, I'm going to retire to a little farm myself. Let me help you, and watch closely." He uncorked the bottle expertly and carried it back to the table, then poured drinks into the three glasses Charlie had brought. All three sipped their wine, Charlie rather tentatively, as he had never tried wine before.

After taking a moment to enjoy his drink, the general said, "Okay, Jerry, let's hear it."

Lieutenant Colonel Martin took a deep breath. "Sir, the Germans aren't certain about Calais, but they are quite certain that Patton will spearhead the invasion. We should use that. Surely the Nazis have spies that report where General Patton is at all times. Why don't you order him to Dover, and build a fake army around him. The Germans will be sure the invasion is coming at Calais, and will move their defenses accordingly."

Ike considered for a moment before saying, "That's an excellent idea, Jerry, an excellent idea. Go on."

"We can send engineers there to build fake tanks, trucks, cannons, barges, everything an invading army would have at its embarkation point. I once read an account of a Confederate General in the Civil War who fooled an entire Union Army into withdrawing from their position by parading the same six cannons and two companies of infantry across a gap in the trees where they could be seen by the Yankees. The troops and cannons marched in a circle, hidden from the Northern troops except when they passed through the gap in the trees again and again. It made them look like a huge force headed to an easily defended position. Maybe we could do the same thing...post a brigade, or maybe just a battalion there and choreograph their movements so it looks like large army. Fake radio traffic, fake couriers to and from SHAEF, all the elements of an army about to attack. What do you think, sir?"

Eisenhower answered immediately, "We'll call it Operation Fortitude. That's a masterful idea, Colonel." His trademark smile brightened the room. "I think you may deserve a promotion...you, too, Charlie." The smile turned to laughter. "Patton as a decoy, sitting in Dover with absolutely nothing to do. He'll be livid. It's perfect. After the Normandy invasion I'll put him in command of 3rd Army...*after* he has had time to become completely contrite. That's wonderful, Jerry."

He thought for a few moments. "I need to assemble senior staff and all of the field commanders." He looked at a calendar on the wall near the bar and did some quick calculations in his head. "If we leak this false information to Collins within the next day or two," he paused, looking at Martin, and asked, "Can you have something believable put together by then, Jerry? Just enough to whet their appetite?" Without waiting for a reply, the General continued, "It'll take about two weeks total for the plan to reach Canais, provide time for his assessment, and return his questions or suggestions to me." After a slight pause he said, "Christmas Eve...we can get together by Christmas Eve. You and Charlie must be there. I'll take care of the rest." The Supreme Allied Commander took another sip of wine and laughed. Through the chortles, he said shakily, "Patton sitting on his keester in Dover. I love it."

Chapter 20

Staff Sergeant Collins took the bait with great excitement. He'd been feeding bits of information to the Abwer for a year, but this was by far the most important report he had ever sent through the intelligence pipeline. The precise location of the Allied invasion. His hands shook as he placed his report into the brown leather envelope and sealed the contents. The envelope would be passed to a courier whom Collins had never met. The system was a simple one. The sergeant would place a small piece of yellow tape in a lower corner of a specific window of a little used room on the first floor of the headquarters building. The window was checked daily, or perhaps more often, by one of the many people who passed by on the outside sidewalk. The small square of yellow tape meant a package would be left under a pillow on one of the plush sofas in a nearby hotel lobby at precisely seven a.m. the next morning. Collins would stop at the hotel on his way to headquarters and sit on the designated sofa reading a newspaper for a few minutes, surreptitiously slipping the envelope under the pillow. He would then leave, and had been advised never to look back or his services to the Abwer would be terminated...possibly violently. Moments later, presumably, the package would be picked up by the courier, who would send it through established channels to the German intelligence high command.

The yellow tape was indicator of a routine message that was not particularly time critical. The sergeant had been instructed to use red tape if the communication was of great importance, but he had never felt the need to do so. Today he would use the red tape.

The rules were different when red tape was the indicator. The staff sergeant was to take the message to the same hotel, making some excuse to allow him time away from his desk, and relax on the same sofa until he was approached by the courier. This was the first time the two would meet, and the sergeant fidgeted nervously as he waited. He looked toward the elevator as the bell announced its arrival at lobby level. The door opened and an elegant woman perhaps fifty years old exited and walked to the reception desk. She conversed with the attendant for few moments before turning and moving deliberately toward Collins.

She held out her hand and said in perfect accent of English gentry, "I am Frou Gruber." Noticing Collins as he looked around nervously, she added while motioning, "We can speak freely here, Herr Sergeant. This hotel is owned by a Dutch business entity that is secretly controlled by the Reich. Many American and British dignitaries stay here, even officers meeting at your headquarters, but all of the hotel staff are trained in espionage, and watch closely who enters. No one enters this building except those whom we wish to be here." She sat down close to Collins. "I am one of several couriers who take your missives and pass them on to Abwer headquarters. The exact mechanism of the transfer is not something of which you need to be aware, but I can tell you that Admiral Canaris is very familiar with your service, and is very pleased with all you have done for the fatherland."

Collins' face registered embarrassment as he said, "Thank you, Frou Gruber." He handed her the envelope. "I shouldn't stay long. This," he waved the envelope, "is the most important information I have ever discovered at SHAEF. It is..."

"Stop!" the lady commanded. "I am a courier... *only* a courier. I have no need to know the nature of the package. It is much better that way in case I am ever discovered and arrested. I pass the intelligence along, that is all. This particular package I will deliver to Herr Canaris personally. Since you and I have met, I shall not return to England. That way you can never compromise me." She waved her hand around. "As for the hotel and the time you have spent here, many come in, as you have, just to relax, perhaps purchase a pastry or coffee at the hotel bar. If you have been observed coming here, it would not be a thing of importance to anyone."

Frou Gruber stood and held out her hand once more. "Goodbye, Sergeant, and thank you for your service to Germany," she said. "We shall not meet again."

—-■-— —■-— —■-— —■-— —-■-— —-■-— —-■-— —-■-— —■-— —-■-— —-■-— —■--

**

Four days later, Admiral Wilhelm Canaris reread Collins' report with growing excitement. Now he knew the exact location of the invasion as well as its leader, and thus the tactics that would likely be used against the German defenses. The only question was when. It would doubtless be soon, but knowledge of the exact date would be important in determining a proper response. He would contact Eisenhower to glean more information and what actions he could take to insure the success of the invading force.

**

Within a week, Eisenhower had confirmation that Staff Sergeant Michael Collins was their spy. Canaris had contacted the General through their usual channels, asking for more details of the landing, and, considering the import of the massive invasion, suggested they find a way to meet to discuss the German intelligence leader's part in the operation. The Admiral was aware of several previous attempts to assassinate der Fuehrer, and had even provided minor assistance in one of the plots. All had failed, prompting Canaris and several other high ranking officers to develop Operation Valkyrie, the next grand plan to eliminate Hitler. German planning was always meticulous, but as might be expected, also agonizingly slow. Valkyrie was months, perhaps even a year, away from implementation, and like everyone else, Canaris was tired of the pointless war and wanted a much quicker resolution.

On Friday, December 17, Admiral Canaris boarded a newly commissioned Type XXI U-boat at a small port north of Bremen. The Admiral was an old submariner from WWI, having commanded U-38, in which he had sunk four ships. For his actions he was awarded the Iron Cross 2nd Class and later the Iron Cross 1st Class. If anyone noticed his departure on the craft they probably would have written it off as a nostalgic cruise. As it was, no one but his driver was even aware of the early morning mission. The U-boat's Captain was an old friend who hated Hitler and the Nazis as much as Canaris, and was happy to be of assistance in this very important project. The Type XXI boat usually had a crew of fifty eight, but could actually be sailed by a crew of eight, as long as no emergencies, deep dives, or combat were part of the mission. By late 1943 it was a simple task to find eight German sailors who were happy to take on a secret mission that might thwart the plans of Hitler and the Nazis, thereby shortening the war.

They traveled two hundred miles west to a designated point, where they were met by an American submarine. Canaris transferred to the Balao-class sub and was taken up the Thames to meet with Eisenhower aboard the HMS Achilles in the same lavish room where Ike had talked with Lieutenant Colonel Martin and Sergeant Bradley.

Eisenhower had decided it was time to be up front with Canaris about their discovery of his spy at SHAEF, both as a rebuke for placing a spy in his personal staff and as warning that any further information he received from the man was, at best, tarnished. The Admiral surprised him by laughing unrestrainedly when he heard of the brilliant ruse that had smoked out his man. He wanted to know every detail of Operation Overlord and of Operation Fortitude as well.

After two hours of discussion it was decided that there were only a few minor areas in which Canaris could help the actual Normandy invasion and subsequent move inland. German defenses would be formidable, but one thing the intelligence chief could accomplish was to see that radio traffic in the area all pointed to the expected attack far to the north at Calais. The main subterfuge to be accomplished by the Admiral would be his report to German High Command of absolute confirmation of a massive invasion force led by General George Patton and focused on the beaches twenty miles either side of Calais. He would report that the exact date of the invasion was not yet determined, but best estimates gave it a time frame of late spring to mid-summer. Canaris was giddy with the idea of the physical structure of a fake army built around Patton at Dunkirk, and would include suggestions in his report that the Luftwaffe could concentrate aerial surveillance on that area to keep High Command apprised of the size and movements of the force.

When the meeting was ended and Admiral Canaris was preparing to board the waiting submarine to make the return trip to Germany, Ike presented him with a case of Miller High Life beer. With his grand trademark smile, he said, "Admiral, I know you Germans think you can brew beer, but I think you should try this. In the States, it's advertised as 'the Champaign of beers,' and I think that says it all."

Canaris took the large box and held it up to his eyes, studying the logo printed on the outside of the cardboard. He returned the General's smile. "Thank you, General Eisenhower. I shall enjoy this. He took a step up the gangway, then turned, the smile still on his face. "You realize, of course, that the Mr. Miller for whom this beer is named was a German brewer who brought his business to America before the Great War erupted in Europe." The Admiral was laughing as he boarded the submarine and handed the box to an American sailor for storage.

After the submarine had gone, Eisenhower picked up the telephone and dialed Lieutenant Colonel Martin's desk. He briefly explained that he had met with the Admiral, and suggested the addition of several other officers to discuss inclusion of this new development into the invasion plan. The two spent several minutes confirming exactly who should be in attendance at the secret meeting. "Jerry, we have a house in Croydon that is a good venue for a meeting of this kind. It's on Grimiwade Avenue, bordering Lloyd Park. Beautiful location and more secluded than headquarters. Let's confirm the date for December 24th, Christmas Eve, at, say, 1100 hours. That will give us time to conclude our business and get everyone back to," he paused for a moment before saying through a bemused chuckle, "back to whatever they had planned for Christmas. Since none of us have family here, we may all spend Christmas together anyway. I'll see you tomorrow, Colonel. I think tonight I'll stay on Mr. Churchill's boat and relax."

Ike hung up the phone, unaware that he had made a rare and grave mistake. By sheer luck, Staff Sergeant Collins had picked up his own telephone, which by coincidence was connected to the same line answered by Lieutenant Colonel Martin. He listened to the entire conversation. Anger racked his body, and his hand shook as he hung up the telephone. He had been discovered and, more humiliating, had been used. Used by Canaris. Used by Eisenhower. He stormed out of his office and out of the building. It was cold and raining outside, and Collins had left without a jacket, but he didn't care. He needed to walk...to think this out...to plan revenge.

Chapter 21

Collins did not return to work that day, and called in sick the next morning. In fact, he *was* sick, but not with anything that could be measured by a doctor or corpsman. He was sickened by the fact he'd been betrayed, and it never once entered his mind that he was, with his traitorous actions, betraying his own countrymen. The sergeant didn't really consider England to be his country. Ireland was his home, and to Ireland was his allegiance. Ireland, his part of it, at least, hated the English, and that hatred justified everything he could do to defeat England and its allies in this war with Germany.

He considered his current situation. He had not been arrested, even though his treachery had been discovered some time ago. That meant Eisenhower thought he could still use the sergeant to funnel information—false information—to the Germans. Today, however, Ike had told Canaris of his knowledge of Collins' activities. Now that the Admiral knew he was compromised, any information he passed along to a courier would be known by German intelligence to be useless. He was useless to Eisenhower and useless to Canaris as well. Yet he had not been arrested as a spy, a traitor. Why?

He had just acquired new intelligence. Real intelligence. Important information. He knew where and when the Allied high command was meeting in supposed secrecy. He knew, for the most part, who would be in attendance. The top brass who would assemble at this meeting in Croydon represented the ultimate command structure of both the British and American Armies. If there was a way to destroy them en mass, to kill them all as they talked about invading Germany, the entire Allied war effort would be crippled. There would be disarray, chaos in the ranks. Hitler could invade England with practically no opposition during the panic caused by lack of Allied leadership. If Collins could orchestrate this, he would be a hero of the Reich. The staff sergeant knew he lacked the knowledge to plan or carry out such a mission, but if he could just start the process, just inform the right person that Canaris was a traitor, that the Allied high command would be seated around a table in Croydon on Christmas Eve, awaiting annihilation, he would be able to write his own ticket in Hitler's Third Reich, to do anything, be anything he wanted.

But how?

Collins entered the barracks he shared with several other noncommissioned officers. The only other Sergeant present stared at him quizzically as he shivered and dripped on the floor, but said nothing. The staff sergeant sullenly grabbed a towel and headed for the showers, where he stripped and immersed himself in the stream of hot water until the chill was gone. While he showered, he continued to consider his options. All the people at the hotel where he made his drops would be associated with the Abwer, with Canaris. He could not take this information to them.

But were they all Abwer? Was there anyone at the hotel he could trust? The only courier he had met had told him the hotel was a central point for German spies. Would they all work for Canaris? Maybe it was worth the risk to find out. He could think of no other option.

After donning dry clothing and a jacket, he grabbed one of the several black umbrellas from a rack near the door and hurried out into the rain toward the German hotel. He entered and walked straight to the reception desk at the back of the lobby, near the elevator.

"I need to speak with an officer in the Luftwaffe," he told the young hotelier who manned the desk.

"Vie Beliebt?" the man posed as a question. (I beg your pardon?)

Collins took a deep breath. He was taking a great chance. "I leave messages periodically here with couriers from the Abwer. You've seen me. I have a *very important* message to leave today...but not to the Abwer." He leaned over the desk into the man's face. "I need to speak to an officer in the Luftwaffe. Surely they have representatives in the intelligence community. I need for you to call someone to talk to me."

The hotelier stared at the sergeant in silence for a long minute, then said curtly, "Ich kann es nicht machen." (I can't do it.) He turned to walk away.

"Okay." Collins shouted. "Okay...I'm a dead man anyway, you know." He started for the door, still speaking, "If you don't want my help for *your* country, then I'll surrender to the Allies and tell them all about this place. They should be here in minutes."

As he reached for the door a shrill voice behind him ordered "Halt! Bieib." Stay.

He turned to see a small, blond man probably in his fifties dressed in an expensive English suit standing inside the open elevator. He walked toward the door very deliberately; metal taps on his heels clicking on the stone floor with the measured beat of a metronome. When the man reached Collins, he held out his hand and said in unaccented English, "I am Herr Jager. Can I be of assistance, Staff Sergeant Collins?"

"Are you Luftwaffe?" Collins asked.

"No."

"Are you Abwer?"

"No."

"Then you can't help me." Collins said with disgust and opened the door.

Herr Jager calmly pulled a Luger pistol from a holster inside his jacket and ordered, "Stop, Herr Collins. I am Gestapo, and I *will* shoot you." As the Sergeant turned, eyes glued to the Luger, the German continued, "I can help you, Herr Collins, and I suspect you can help me." He indicated the same sofa where the

Sergeant left his envelopes for the couriers. "Please, Sergeant, have a seat. Let us speak civilly."

"How do I know you're Gestapo?" Collins asked.

Jager only shrugged. "It's a fair question, Sergeant. One to which I have no answer that will convince you." He subtly shifted the Lugar until it was pointing at Collins once more. "Rather than me convincing you of who I am, why don't you convince me that you have information of value to the Gestapo...or to the Luftwaffe for that matter. You don't have to trust me implicitly. You don't have to tell me the entire story, only enough to convince me to take you to my superiors."

Collins thought for a moment, quickly realizing he wasn't in a position to make demands. "I have some information about Admiral Canaris...personal information that would be of interest to the High Command."

"Canaris?" Jager raised his eyebrows, He smiled, then asked, "And why the Luftwaffe?"

"The information will be *very* interesting to the Luftwaffe, Herr Jager. It could provide solutions to many problems. I can say nothing more."

Jager smiled as he placed the pistol back into the holster. "Come with me, Herr Sergeant. There are some very interesting people I would like you to meet."

Providing no further explanation, the German turned and walked toward a stairwell near the elevator. Collins waited only a brief moment before quickly following. They walked down three flights of stairs, finally entering a well appointed room with no windows, the only entrance to which was the door from the stairwell. "Please, make yourself comfortable, Herr Sergeant," he said, motioning around the room. "There is a phonograph and many books. You will have a wait of a few hours." As the Sergeant stepped into the room, Jager closed the door without entering. There was a click as he engaged the lock. Collins tried the door, and realized he was a prisoner, possibly of the Gestapo, possibly of the Abwer, possibly of just about anyone. He plopped glumly into one of the plush chairs and stared at the wall.

There was no clock, but after what must have been several hours, there was a rattling at the door as it was unlocked. Collins watched as the door opened and Herr Jager entered along with a very young man in a Luftwaffe uniform with Leutnant (second lieutenant) shoulder boards. "Herr Collins, here is your Luftwaffe officer," Jager said as if with pride. "Leutnant Hans Steiger." The young officer stared passively at the sergeant, saying nothing, as Jager continued, "Leutnant Steiger does not have the authority to listen to your story, but he will fly you to someone who does. We have been waiting for dusk so you may travel with safety." Both men turned to leave as Jager said, "Please follow."

After a three hour trip by automobile, with the Leutnant driving, the three men arrived at grass field surrounded by woods somewhere south of London. The field was just long enough to support take offs and landings by small aircraft, and sitting at one end was a Siebel Si 204 light transport aircraft. The twin engine craft had room for eight passengers as well as the pilot and copilot. For this flight, however, Leutnant Steiger would be alone at the controls with Collins as the only passenger.

As the boarded the craft, the staff sergeant asked, "How did a German aircraft get here? And, for that matter, where are we going?"

"Where are *you* going, Herr Sergeant," Jager answered with a cruel smile. "I shall remain here. To answer your first question, the Leutnant is an excellent pilot. He flew across the Channel two nights ago at an extremely low altitude to stay under the British coastal radar. He regularly transports agents and communications to and from Germany for an intelligence network that is," he formulated his words carefully before continuing, "outside the sphere of the Abwer. Fog kept him from returning to Germany last night, so it was our good fortune that he was planning to return tonight. He will take you across the Channel tonight, and you will meet with some people who will assure you of my identity." The cruel smile never left his face as he spoke.

The flight, for Collins at least, was terrifying. They flew without lights, in total darkness, at an altitude of a hundred feet or less across the English Channel. Strong winds near the surface were finally breaking up the low cloud cover that had brought cold rain to the west coast of England for several days. The wind came from the north, which was directly off of the port wing with their westerly direction of flight, and buffeted the small craft with strong gusts every few minutes. Occasionally the moonlight would break through the clouds, illuminating the whitecaps rising from the rough water of the Channel that seemed to be only feet below them. Collins could swear that on several occasions he heard and felt ocean spray hitting the bottom of the aircraft. He was sitting in the first passenger row behind and to the right of Leutnant Steiger, and could see the man's face clearly anytime the moonlight peeked into the cabin. The sergeant took some comfort in the fact that his pilot appeared to be calm, possibly even enjoying the very rough flight. Collins had not eaten lunch or dinner, and the queasy sensation in his stomach reminded him that he was glad of that fact.

Two and a half hours of being beaten around in the sky brought them to a small airfield north of Paris, where they were met by a staff car and three rough looking men in black leather trench coats. They put Collins in the back seat and drove without speaking into the city, finally stopping at an ancient downtown building that housed offices of the German High Command.

They walked up two flights of stairs, then down a wide hallway lined on both sides by ancient suits of armor and paintings of French nobility. At the end of the hall the men stopped at an elaborately carved double door and knocked.

After a few moments, the door was opened by another, much younger, German dressed entirely in black, with a Waffen SS insignia on the collar of his shirt, but no indication of rank. He said nothing, but motioned for Collins to enter the room. The sergeant's three guides or captors, whichever they were, remained outside as the door closed. The silent young man led Collins across the large drawing room, doubtless designed for French royalty in a time long past, until they reached the large Louis XIV desk near a stained glass window. Staff Sergeant Collins took a sharp breath as the man behind the table looked up at him. Anyone in Europe, in 1943, would recognize the face of Heinrich Himmler, Hitler's chief henchman and Reichsführer of the Schutzstaffel (SS).

Himmler stared at the sergeant in silence for several agonizing minutes. His black, piercing eyes, staring through wire rimmed spectacles, had a paralyzing effect on the Brit, and there was a long moment when Collins ceased to breathe. Finally, the Reichsfuhrer said in slow English, as if he had memorized the line, "I am told you require confirmation of the identity of my agent in London." He stared directly into the shaking Sergeant's eyes, awaiting a response.

"Sir, I apologize," Collins began, his voice quavering, "I have very important information that couldn't get into the wrong hands." Himmler looked at him questioningly for a few seconds before turning to the young man in black, who translated the sergeant's words.

As understanding dawned on Himmler's face, he said, again in measured English, "Ah, yes. Important information." He paused, his eyes once more drilling into those of the British sergeant. "And do you trust *me* to receive information of such great importance?"

Collins began for the first time to question the sagacity of his working relationship with the Germans. Himmler's round face, wire rimmed glasses, and receding hairline made him look unassuming and plebian. In another uniform and another age, he could easily have been mistaken for an accountant or a college professor. Except for those eyes...those black, penetrating eyes that captivated one to look deeply into them only to find that the only thing they reflected was pure evil.

In his position at SHAEF, the staff sergeant had read several reports regarding atrocities Hitler and his commanders had committed on the people of the countries they had overrun. The Jews, particularly, had been herded into concentration camps and treated inhumanely, a fact that added much urgency to the Allies hopes to destroy Hitler's Reich and return Europe to sanity. The sergeant had no way of knowing, however, that the man before whom he stood had been responsible for the horrific extermination of millions of Jewish, Romanian, and Soviet civilians, as well as countless other groups. He had no way of knowing...no one did...that Himmler and his regime would kill between twelve and fourteen million harmless and helpless noncombatants before the war ended.

What Collins did know was that Himmler's eyes instilled in him a fear such as he had never encountered, never in his most frightening nightmares. He swallowed hard, suddenly realizing that he had no choice but to tell all to the monster before him. He feared for his life, but at the same time he realized that his life was over. This evil would kill him as soon as his usefulness was at an end, and he was powerless to do anything about it.

For the next thirty minutes, Collins explained how he had been passing intelligence to Admiral Canaris through the system of couriers based in the hotel near Allied Headquarters. He spoke directly to Himmler, who frequently stopped the sergeant in order to turn to his assistant for translation and to allow time for him to make notes. Occasionally the Reichsfuehrer asked a question through his translator, but mostly he only listened. Upon hearing of the Admiral's crossing of the Channel to meet with Eisenhower, Himmler had grunted a sound of disgust and engaged in a protracted conversation in German with his translator, none of which was understood by Collins. The sergeant had no way of knowing that Himmler was already investigating Admiral Canaris for his probable involvement with at least one assassination attempt on der Fuehrer. Himmler had, in fact, been looking for an excuse to arrest the Admiral, but had not yet discovered enough proof to convince Hitler of the treachery the head of the Abwer had instigated, and continued to do so, against the Reich and der Fuehrer personally. Perhaps this British turncoat sergeant held the key to the old Admiral's arrest.

The Reichsfuehrer returned his piercing stare to the Brit, but betrayed no emotion. He personally despised traitors from *any* army, but realized their usefulness as long as their treachery was not directed against him.

After listening to Collins' lengthy explanation, Himmler actually smiled at the man, and said, "Thank you, Sergeant. You may go." He pressed an unseen button, artfully placed into the burled wood carving of the desk, prompting the double doors to open and the same three men who had brought the sergeant to enter the office. They briskly and wordlessly escorted Collins from the office and closed the doors.

Staff Sergeant Michael Collins was never seen again.

After the men had departed, Himmler ordered his assistant, "Get Reichsmarschal Goring on the telephone. The British sergeant was correct. As commander of the Luftwaffe, Goring will be extremely interested in this information. Perhaps he can orchestrate a little surprise for this Christmas Eve meeting of the Allied leadership."

As the young man moved to pick up the telephone on his own desk, Himmler added, "And Karl...when you are finished, bring me the Canaris file."

Chapter 21

Turning up his collar against the wind, Jack walked briskly toward the squadron commander's office. He was wishfully thinking that maybe some transportation had been authorized that would get him back to the states earlier than expected. It was cold and windy out, but the rain had finally broken, and blue sky was visible for the first time in several days through the ever enlarging holes between the clouds. He reached up to hold onto his garrison cap as a wind gust almost blew it off of his head.

Major Isaacson was on the telephone as Jack entered, so the airman stood at attention in front of the officer's desk until the call ended.

"At ease, airman," said the major, then "It's good to see you, Jack." He chuckled, "You're getting famous all over England, you know."

"Sir?" the veteran gunner questioned.

Isaacson explained, "A bird colonel from Supply and Acquisition called this morning. He offered to give us a dozen turkeys and as many hams, with sweet potatoes and cranberry sauce as trimming, for our Christmas dinner, with one condition. That will certainly beat the hell out of the Brussels sprouts and mutton we had planned."

"Wow!" Jack, surprised at the Christmas fare, was disappointed that this conversation probably had nothing to do with his going home. "What do you mean, one condition, sir?"

The Major smiled broadly and answered, "Like I said, you're getting famous all over England. Their condition is you have to go pick up the food in person. They all want to meet you before you go home. It's only ninety miles, about a three hour drive over some of those roads, to Guildford, the distribution warehouse for most of our food. Guildford is southwest of London. Command moved it there to escape the nightly bombings in London proper." He laughed, "You know, they used to tell us they were planning to send us *good* food, but it was blown up by the Germans, so they sent what they had. Now I guess they'll have to find a new excuse." He paused, still smiling, "It's interesting, but completely understandable that the top brass thinks it's okay for the Germans to bomb SHAEF headquarters in London on a nightly basis, but it's important to protect the food at all costs."

Jack was laughing, too. "I can see that, sir. We can do without leadership a lot better than we can do without three squares a day." When it dawned on him what he had just said to the officer, the airman's face dropped and he was immediately contrite. "Sorry, sir, I was just..."

"It's okay, Jack. I understand," the CO said. "Often I even agree. It's December 23rd. Why don't you grab your buddy Lancaster, requisition a Carry All from the motor pool, and drive to the warehouse this afternoon. You can stay the night, have dinner with all the guys so they can brag to their grandchildren about how they met you," he smiled as he noticed Jack's face redden, "and bring back the goodies tomorrow. That will give the cook plenty of time to see if he can make turkey and sweet potatoes taste like mutton and Brussels sprouts."

Jack thought for just a moment before answering, "Sure...okay, Major, I can do that." He saluted, and turned to leave.

"Have a good trip," he heard the CO say as he went out the door.

Two hours later Jack and Freddy were slipping and slogging through a muddy bog that was once a road west of London. Paved roads had been available along their route, but all looked extremely busy, with traffic tie-ups and frequent complete stoppages, so the adventurous duo decided to take a less traveled route, one represented only by a curved set of dashes on their map. The WC-53 Carry All they had requisitioned was basically an enclosed pick-up truck that served a multitude of purposes in the Army...squad sized troop movement, ambulance, delivery of a variety of materials and ordinance, hence the name Carry All. It was lightweight, and only a two-wheel drive vehicle, which made moving through heavy mud a difficult task. The two and a half hour trip predicted by Major Isaacson was closer to five hours in total, but finally the mud covered truck and its pair of wet and tired drivers made it to the warehouse.

Even with their CO's warning, the two were not prepared for their welcome as celebrities. Nasty and mud covered as they were, they walked up to a master sergeant standing at the door to the warehouse who stared at them with disgust until they introduced themselves. He broke into a broad smile and said, "Well, now, the colonel's orders were to bring you directly to his office when you arrived."

Jack and Freddie begged the master sergeant to allow them time to clean up, but the veteran soldier said with a wry grin, "Orders are orders, men."

The two were fed a sumptuous dinner and endured what seemed like hundreds of handshakes and pats on the back. Jack was asked several times to describe shooting down German fighters, and both men were questioned incessantly about their crash and harrowing escape from Germany. At one point Freddy said to Jack, "Man, I feel like you're Captain Glenn Miller and I'm his Army Air Force Band. On second thought, I'll bet they aren't treated this well."

It was mid morning the next day that the truck was finally loaded with the generous Christmas meal donated by the men of the supply depot, and the two airmen started on their way. Only a short discussion was required to reach a decision to take the main roads back to Boreham, regardless of traffic. Their route took them through Sutton and into Croydon, on the southern outskirts of London. The roads were paved, thank goodness, and the traffic was relatively light until they reached the western edge of Croydon. A group of

American MP's were posted at a major intersection to advise traffic of a makeshift detour.

A large fire had broken out in the warehouse district, which was along their route, and made passage on the narrow highway unsafe. They were directed to travel southeast down Coombe Road for a few miles where another group of MPs would direct them through a residential neighborhood until they could safely rejoin the highway. As was often the case, military communication was lacking in specifics, and five miles later they were stopped at the outpost that was to direct them further.

"We're headed to Boreham Airfield, just the other side of Chelmsford," Freddy told the British Corporal who was apparently in charge. The man was actually Australian, the fact of which was readily apparent when he answered with an Antipodean, "Sorry, mate, but you can't go east from here. It's a restricted area."

"But the fire is miles to the north," Jack commented. "Why is travel restricted way down here?"

"Ain't got nothin' to do with the fire, mate," answered the Aussie. "I can't tell you any more than that."

Freddy's eyes were suddenly bright. "Hey, Corporal, do you have any idea who this is?" he asked, pointing to Jack. "This man is the one who holds the record for downed German fighters by any bomb group gunner."

The Australian looked surprised, then stared quizzically at Jack. "Crykies, mate. Are you the one what shot down those two hundred Germans in just twenty missions?"

Jack looked embarrassed. "It wasn't that many, but, yeah, I'm the guy." He indicated toward the back of the Carry All. "Supply depot over in Guildford gave us some turkeys to celebrate Christmas and my going home. They wanted to meet me, so Freddy and me drove there last night to pick up the food." He gazed longingly down the eastern road. "Looks like we're not going to get them back to the cook in time."

The Corporal looked thoughtful for a moment, finally saying, "Tell you what, mate. If you let me shake your hand, I'll jump in the truck with you and do my hourly 'inspection' of the restricted route. When we get to the other end, you can go on your way, and I'll get one of the blokes from that guard post to bring me back. How does that sound to you?"

"Great," both men answered as Jack held out his hand to his Australian ally. "Thanks, Corporal."

Less than ten minutes later the three men were driving slowly past a large Elizabethan style mansion, the driveway and curb of which was crowded with military staff cars bearing emblems of several different Allied Armies. The corporal said softly, "Meeting of all the bigwigs. That's the reason for the restrictions." He shook his head. "There's enough brass in there to make bullets for the whole Australian Army, mate," he said without cracking a smile, then added, "maybe your Army, too. Stop and let me out. I need to make a quick patrol around the building, then I'll be right back." As he spoke, air raid sirens could be heard in the distance, toward London, and at the same time the drone of large aircraft engines could be heard overhead. Jack and Freddy looked up nervously then glanced at the Corporal.

"Don't worry, mates," he said calmly. "Those are Heinkels out of Saint Lo. They pass over here almost every day on their way to bomb London. They're not interested in Croydon."

As the Australian was speaking, three bombers broke off from the German squadron and rapidly dropped altitude for a bomb run on Croydon. Reichsmarschell Goring had received Himmler's message, and had instructed his Air Marshalls to bomb the specific street address provided by Sergeant Collins at the specific time of the meeting. The Heinkel bombers came in at an altitude of only one thousand feet, and thus were guaranteed to hit the large structure, hopefully with several bombs, to ensure that all of the leaders would perish in the conflagration.

Jack had begun to answer the corporal when the truck was suddenly hurled into the air; the violent movement followed a millisecond later by a loud and fiery blast coming from the direction of the mansion. The truck landed on its side, all three occupants momentarily addled by the blast and the crash onto the pavement. Explosions were all around them shaking the ground. Freddy could smell gasoline leaking somewhere around the truck, and began to drag a partially conscious Jack from the wreck. After pulling his companion away to the relative safety of a shallow ditch, he returned to the truck for the Australian. Jack flinched as a bomb exploded just the other side of the Carry All, and stuck his head up just in time to watch in horror as the truck exploded with both the Corporal and his good friend Freddy inside. The fireball ensured that no one survived.

Across the street, the large block turret topped with battlements and arrow ports that formed one corner of mansion, had partially collapsed along with a major portion of the front of the brick and stone structure. The air was filled with black smoke from the explosions and fires, limiting visibility to almost nothing, but Jack watched as the faint image of a man crawling from the rubble screamed, "Anyone out there? I need help. General Eisenhower and the others are trapped!" The man collapsed, then struggled to his feet once more. Jack crawled from the ditch, taking one more look at the burning truck and deciding there was nothing he could do for his friend, moved unsteadily toward the mansion. As he approached the tall, thin man dropped to his knees in shock.

"Charlie?" he asked in a weak, dreamlike voice. "Charlie Bradley?"

Charlie stared at the airman before him. It was only when he looked into the man's eyes that he asked, "Jack?" The two men embraced, both with tears in their eyes at the thought of this chance meeting, until almost in unison they considered the situation around them. The bombers had left, but the devastation behind them was worsening. Portions of the mansion were on fire. Other parts were fully or partially collapsed, and more threatened to come down at any minute.

"Jack, they're all in there!" Charlie said with panic in his voice. "Ike, Churchill, Smith, Bradley, Montgomery...all the rest. Some important-looking civilians I didn't recognize. They're trapped, under the rubble, maybe dead. We need to do something."

Jack looked at his friend. The ankle of his left leg was twisted at an odd angle and blood was soaking through the pants leg on the right side. "Charlie, let me go see what I can inside. You're hurt. Bleeding. Stay here."

As Charlie voiced objections, Jack left him and ran toward the house. The large double front doors were crushed, but a broken window on one side of the structure offered access into the mansion. Jack climbed through and walked in a crouch as far as he could, then crawled through rubble until he reached a large room near the center that was relatively intact but for an outside wall that had been blown in by an outside blast. Bricks, glass, tables, chairs, and bodies had been thrown about. The bodies all seemed to carry general's stars on their shoulder boards...*lots* of general's stars. Jack thought grimly about what the Australian had said, "Enough brass to make bullets for the Australian Army." It was too much, and the young soldier was on the verge of panic as he looked around at so much destruction with no idea what to do.

Pieces of stone trim suddenly fell from the ceiling, followed a moment later by the entire ceiling dropping about two feet. This building is coming down soon, Jack thought. He grabbed the body nearest the gaping hole in the wall and dragged the man to a point where he had to lift him out the hole and to the ground. The body was that of a British General. He was breathing shallowly, but was unconscious and two hundred fifty pounds of dead weight, and the five foot six inch airman struggled to drag him a safe distance from the destruction. As Jack re-entered through the hole, he noticed Charlie crawling into the other side of the room. He stood shakily, still limping on his obviously broken ankle and still with blood seeping from this right leg.

"I can help," he said weakly, and immediately went to a tall body under one of the tables. "General Eisenhower. Can you hear me?" he shouted. Ike's eyes opened momentarily, and seemed to recognize Sergeant Bradley, but quickly closed as he lapsed into unconsciousness. Blood was seeping from his right temple. Through the swirling dust and settling debris, Charlie craned his neck looking for help. Spotting a figure coming through the window, he shouted, "Jack. This is General Eisenhower. Help me get him out." The two men dragged the Supreme Allied Commander across the floor and out of the building as even more bricks fell from the wall. They re-entered six times, each time dragging out one of the high ranking planners of Operation Overlord. Jack recognized

General Omar Bradley, Churchill, and Montgomery from photographs he had seen, but others were not familiar to him.

On the unlucky seventh trip, with Charlie becoming pale and unsteady from blood loss, the ceiling collapsed. Jack's legs were pinned under a large steel beam, and Charlie appeared to have been crushed under a mountain of debris and heavy furniture that dropped from a second floor room. Jack was conscious but couldn't see or move his legs beneath the beam and debris. He felt around for anything that might be used as a pry bar finally feeling what turned out to be an M-14 rifle, probably from one of the guards. The airman couldn't remember seeing an enlisted man in the room, but quickly dismissed the thought. He wiggled the rifle from the debris pile and maneuvered it between his legs and the steel beam. With the thick wooden stock under the beam and the rifle barrel pointed toward his face as he lay there, he pushed with all his might, and felt the pressure slightly relieve off his legs. He wiggled with his butt and elbows, and was able to move perhaps a foot before he could no longer hold the rifle barrel. Repositioning the rifle and with two more similar moves, the airman was finally free. Both his legs were bleeding at thigh level, one of them profusely. Since he always carried a folding pocketknife, he pulled a tablecloth near enough to cut a portion of it for a bandage, which he tied around the most serious wound.

Jack crawled under the collapsed ceiling to where he had last seen Charlie, and finally found his friend buried under a pile of debris that may have been the only support left. He didn't care. As carefully as he could, sometimes laying on his belly and moving chunks of lumber and concrete by hand, he freed Charlie and began the laborious process of dragging him from the room through an opening that was now scarcely eighteen inches tall. Charlie was unconscious but breathing, and Jack assumed help would be there quickly, so he returned once more to the house. He could remember the location of at least five more people in the room, and would do what he could to get them out before the entire house fell on them.

As he reached the small opening in the brick wall, Jack glanced back at the group of bodies he and Charlie had dragged to a spot under a large oak tree. He wondered for a brief moment why there were not hundreds of soldiers converging on the spot where their highest leadership had just been attacked by the enemy. Then he remembered. The meeting was secret. No one knew. It was possible that even the guards at either end of the road had no idea of whom they were guarding. If only the Australian Corporal knew who was in the mansion, he was dead, and couldn't summon help. Jack looked once more at the bodies under the tree and wondered if he was doing any good by dragging more people out of the house. It was possible he was only moving them to die in another place.

Nonetheless, the soldier steeled himself to crawl into the small opening once more, grimacing as he did so at the steady stream of dust and pea-sized debris that fell continuously on him from the floors above. Small debris likely portended much larger pieces not far behind. A shoe protruded from a pile to his left. He grabbed it and moved his hand past the laces far enough to ascertain there was a foot attached to the shoe.

Almost a half hour was required to move enough pieces of lumber, brick, and other detritus to clear the chest, and finally the head of the victim. The dress was civilian. The clothing and face were covered in grey dust to such a degree that recognition of the person was impossible, but Jack did note blood seeping from wounds about the head and neck, mixing with the dust to form black rivulets that ran onto the floor. The airman had no medical training, but he was pretty certain dead people don't bleed, so the fact that this man's wounds were still seeping was a somewhat positive sign. He grabbed the man's ankle with his left hand and backed on his belly toward the opening, hoping all the while that it had not collapsed while he was digging.

Two more trips through the hole, two more bodies recovered. One was civilian, the other an American Brigadier General who was unfamiliar to Jack. The Brigadier may not have been alive, but much as he had done as a waist gunner in battle, the airman had reached a point he was in a kind of shock, and performing on 'automatic pilot,' as Lieutenant Holland had called it.

Jack thought he heard the sound of approaching trucks as he stood before the tiny opening one more time. He was pushing his luck, but maybe the upper floors of the mansion would remain upper floors long enough for him to drag out one more body. He crawled on his belly through the once large hole. Twenty feet into the room a heavy wooden table had supported the ceiling. Under the table lay a man in a nicely tailored English suit with a crest of some kind on the jacket pocket. His face, and the jacket were dirty, but his eyes were open. "Have you come to save me?" he asked in a stately British accent. "

"I have, sir," Jack answered. "Are you hurt?"

"I am not certain," the man answered, looking up and down his body, "but I think not." Not much could be seen beyond the legs of the table, but he looked intently all around. "Are there other injured who need assistance before me?"

"I don't know," Jack answered. "Charlie and I have moved several from the room. There may be others, but you're next, sir. Let's go before the whole house comes down. If you're not hurt, maybe you can help me with the next ones."

Jack helped the man from under the table, and crawled beside him as they reached the more collapsed part of the ceiling. Half way across the room, perhaps fifteen feet from the opening in the wall, a rumbling started and Jack could feel more debris falling on his back. He instinctively threw himself on top of the civilian, covering the man's head and neck under his abdomen as he tried to maintain a position of 'hands and knees' against the pressure that was building on his back. The third floor had collapsed into the already fallen second, allowing the outside brick wall and the roof to cave in and entrap the two men under tons of brick, mortar, and steel.

Several minutes later, a British accented voice asked, "Young man, are you alive?"

There was no answer.

Chapter 23

Jack awoke on January 6. He had spent two days trapped under the rubble of the Croydon mansion, along with the companion whom he had covered as the floors and walls fell. The companion's injuries, thanks to the airman's heroic action, were quite minor— scrapes, cuts, bruises, and a greenstick fracture of one ankle that occurred when a large granite block fell on it. Jack's injuries were much more serious. His legs, already injured from shrapnel during the bombing, had both been broken by the same granite block that broke the ankle of the civilian with him. Most serious, however, was the head wound caused by a steel beam that had hit directly on the side of his head, shattering the parietal bone and pushing the shards inward to create pressure on his brain. A surgical team had spent hours removing bits of bone, piece by tiny piece, then replacing it with a metal plate that would allow the brain to rebound into its normal shape after the swelling subsided. How much permanent damage had been done was something that would not be determined for several months, if not years.

Friends from his squadron, along with soldiers from all across England who didn't know him, but had heard of his shooting record, had come to visit during the time he was in the hospital. He didn't remember, and would never remember those twelve days immediately after the bombing, which coincided precisely with the Twelve Days of Christmas, 1943. According to doctors and visitors, he had been awake and alert for the entire time, occasionally lapsing into nonsensical chatter but usually conversing in a normal manner, but simply had no memory of any of it. His visitors had included hundreds of enlisted men, along with Generals Dwight Eisenhower, Beetle Smith, Sir Bernard Law Montgomery, and several other planners of what would become the D-Day Invasion. Sergeant Charlie Bradley came to the London hospital every day. His Colonel, Jerald Martin, was one of the few left in the meeting room of the mansion as the building collapsed, and he did not survive the attack. Charlie now worked directly for General Eisenhower, and Ike had ordered him to visit the hospital daily and bring reports of Jack's condition to the desk of the Supreme Allied Commander.

Even after awakening on January 6, Jack remembered none of it.

When the pall lifted from his memory, the first thing he saw was Charlie Bradley sitting in a straight backed chair beside his hospital bed. Jack looked around the room, uncertain of where he was and afraid his mind was playing tricks on him. He hadn't seen his old friend Charlie since the last days of basic training. How could he be here? For that matter, where was 'here' anyway?

"Charlie?" he asked tentatively. "Charlie Bradley? Is that really you?"

"Yeah, Jack, it's me," Charlie answered while grabbing his crutches and struggling out of the chair. "How 'ya doing this morning, buddy? You sure look better. You're eyes are brighter than they have been; you look much better...except for that Arab turban you're wearing, of course."

Jack reached up and was surprised to feel the thick bandage around his head and covering his left eye. "What's going on, Charlie? Where are we? Why am I all bandaged up, and why are you on crutches?"

"We're in a hospital in London, Jack." Charlie looked questioningly at his friend. "Don't you remember? I've been here to visit you every day, and you've had many other visitors. Don't you remember any of it?"

Too distracted by his injuries to think about past visitors, Jack continued to explore the thick bandage on his head. He smiled at his old friend and said, "You're pulling my leg, right Charlie? I haven't seen you since that day in basic when they sent me to California. I'm either dreaming, or nuts, or someone dropped a bomb on my head so I wouldn't remember anything." He reached out to touch his friend, to make certain he was real. "How have you been, buddy? And where have you been? Did you finally get to be a company clerk?"

"Kind of," Charlie answered with a grin. "And you're pretty close to right about that bomb dropping on your head." He further explained, "I work for Eisenhower at SHAEF, but we talked about that a few days ago. You've been bombing Germany and crash landing in B-17s while I've been shuffling papers for the Supreme Allied Commander. You really don't remember? Ike even came here to visit you a few days ago."

"Ike? General Dwight Eisenhower came to visit *me?*" Jack asked, incredulous.

"It's true." Charlie confirmed. "You've really been out of it, haven't you? Let me fill in the last two weeks for you." Charlie proceeded to tell his friend about the bombing in Croydon, leaving out the reason for the meeting of such high level military leaders. From what he personally remembered along with pieces of the story added by others, he explained how the two of them had met in front of the collapsing mansion, how they had dragged several survivors from the rubble, and how Jack had acted alone after Charlie had been knocked unconscious and trapped under the falling debris. He left out the part about Jack and the civilian being trapped under tons of rubble for two days before rescuers could reach them. "We picked one hell of a time for a reunion, Jack," he said, "but I'm glad you showed up when you did."

Jack was silent for a long time, finally saying, "That's quite a story, Charlie. I don't remember any of it."

"Probably a good thing," Charlie said. "I *do* remember a lot of it, and it keeps me up at night. I'll tell you this, though," he smiled broadly. "It's not nearly as good a story as the one you told me and a bunch of guys from your squadron a few nights ago. You knew us, and you looked normal and alert, but you sure were out of it."

"What story?" Jack asked.

"You remember the Campbell Chicks?" Charlie asked.

"Sure."

"Well, you were telling us a story about the time the Chicks were playing the Chicago Cubs back in 1940. The way you told the story, you were flying in formation in a B-17 named 'Hitler's Headache' when your pilot noticed a ball game below and dropped down out of the clouds to take a closer look."

Jack raised the one eyebrow that was not covered by the bandage, but said nothing.

"It was the Chicks playing the Cubs, but the Chicks had some guest players. I was on the team, you said, along with a guy named Freddy Lancaster. Babe Ruth, Stan Musial, Dizzy Dean, and Joe DiMaggio were all on the team, along with the usual Chick's roster except for you, since you were up in the B-17. According to your story, the Chicks were losing badly because the Cubs were cheating. It made everyone in your formation mad."

Jack was wide eyed, at least with his one exposed eye. "What happened?" he asked.

Charlie smirked, "It was *your* story, Jack. We asked you exactly that. What happened, Jack?"

"You answered very matter-of-factly, 'We waited 'till the Cubs were all in their dugout, then we dropped a bomb on them, of course!'" Charlie exploded in laughter. We all laughed 'til we cried, but you were as serious as a fox in a chicken coop. I think you were even offended that we laughed at your story." He slapped his hand on his leg reflexively, then flinched at the pain through his laughter. "Man, you sure were out of it." Suddenly he looked more serious, and said, "Hey, Jack, I'm glad you're back with us."

The two old friends spent the next hour reminiscing and catching up for real. Jack would remember the conversation and all that followed, but would never be burdened with the memory of the bombing, the collapsing mansion, or the two days spent trapped under the rubble.

One other visitor who came twice during the airman's period of amnesia was a distinguished man about Jack's height, who came late at night when the hospital staff was minimal. He was a friendly man with a slight stutter, who always engaged Jack in conversation about American baseball and asked questions about his life in the small farming community of his youth. Each time he left, the stately Brit said, "Thank you, airman. Thank you for your service to your country, to England, and to the Royal Family." Jack remembered none of it.

Over the next months, as the commanding generals pieced together the events of December 23rd, Jack and Charlie were often subjects of the conversation. They discussed the possibility of medals for the pair, possibly even recommending Jack for the

Medal of Honor. He certainly deserved it. Perhaps they both did.

There were still a few months before the D-Day Invasion, however, and public knowledge of the meeting of so many high level military leaders would certainly portend something extremely important if, as they certainly would, details of the clandestine assembly became public along with the awarding of medals of valor. The Germans were not stupid. They knew an invasion was coming, and because of the influence of Admiral Canaris, believed the ruse of Patton leading the charge to Calais from Dunkirk.

Knowledge of the meeting at Croydon, and realization that Patton was absent from the group, would make the German High Command question the validity of their intelligence. This was one of those rare circumstances, they all agreed, where meritorious service above and beyond the call of duty should be forgotten in lieu of secrecy to protect the war effort.

Luckily for them, when Jack awakened on January 6th, the last thing he remembered was pulling up to the guard shack on Coombe Road and being escorted down a residential street by an Australian Corporal. The airman had a vague recollection of his friend Freddy dying in a burning truck, a remembrance that would wake him in the middle of the night for decades after the war, but he could not remember any specifics or anything at all about what happened next.

Jack didn't remember meeting his old friend Charlie; he didn't remember pulling Ike, or Churchill, or any of the others from the debris of the falling house. He didn't remember, would never know, that the civilian whom he had protected with his body as the house collapsed on top of them was George VI, the King of England.

Jack would remain in military and VA hospitals for two years, and after recovery from his wounds would live a normal life with no evidence of diminished capacity of any kind. He would never remember the days immediately after his injuries...never remember his heroic actions preceding the Twelve Days of Christmas, 1943.

In mid-February of 1944, Jack was shipped to a stateside hospital, where he would remain for more than a year. After much discussion at SHAEF, his injuries, along with the death of Sergeant Lancaster, were reported to the commander of the 925th Aviation Engineers and the CO of the 92nd Bombardment Group as the result of a vehicle accident. Jack and Freddie were recorded as the first casualties to be suffered by the 925th Engineer Aviation Regiment. The actual street address of the incident was listed as that of the mansion in Croydon, but there was no mention of Operation Overlord or the bombing that took place there.

By the time of the D-Day Invasion, the incident was all but forgotten.

After almost two years in military hospitals and convalescent centers, Jack came home early in 1945 to begin rebuilding his life. Doctors from the Veteran's

Administration hospital where he had spent the last several months before his discharge had told him he should never attempt to work again. He would be provided with a monthly military disability check that would provide living expenses. They told him it was his country's way of thanking him for his sacrifice.

The former airman thought that was a completely ridiculous proposition. He didn't feel disabled...he was *not* disabled in any meaningful sense, and would work wherever and at whatever he chose. He accepted his military discharge with glee, and was happy to put the Army Air Corps, the VA, and any other kind of government control of his life behind him. The young civilian went home, found a job working for a small lumber company, asked a wonderful lady named Hazel to be his wife, and settled down to the small town life he had missed during his time away.

Chapter 24

Charlie Bradley's career followed that of his boss, General Dwight D. Eisenhower. Ike became Army Chief of Staff after the war ended, and basically oversaw the mustering out of eight million combatants, leaving a standing Army of only one million by 1948. Charlie Bradley was at his side as an administrator, and hoped to move with him as he became head of NATO in 1950. Eisenhower had been approached by mid-1950 by people of importance who wanted him to be a candidate for U.S. President in the 1952 election.

Ike was quite fond of Charlie Bradley, and saw great potential in the young man, especially if he could obtain a more formal education. The general ordered his young charge to Boston in 1950 and arranged for tutors to complete his high school education to a point that Charlie could obtain admission to Harvard University. It took only a year for the bright young man to gain acceptance to the prestigious university, especially with a recommendation from Dwight Eisenhower, and only three years of intense study to obtain a degree in business administration. Ike was in the middle of his first term as President of the United States by then, and was overjoyed when Charlie joined his staff in an unnamed advisory position.

The President had offered his young friend a prestigious position as Undersecretary of any Cabinet office he chose, but Charlie preferred to be unfettered by the formal chain of command, and asked his boss if he could serve as a 'freelance' advisor, basically a highly placed lackey to do the president's bidding.

Ike laughed at the idea, but liked it. Within weeks, much to the consternation of several members of the senior presidential staff, Charlie was one of only a small handful of people in Washington, D. C. who could come into the president's office unannounced practically any time he chose. He was a valuable advisor, offering positions on several national issues that reflected both his military and administrative experience, but also, and possibly more importantly, reflecting the thought processes of youth. Most of the president's Cabinet and other advisors were his own age or older. They had valuable experience from which to draw, but Eisenhower realized from working with young officers throughout the war that young people thought differently, had not yet been corrupted by the demands of their superiors, and often had insights into a variety of problems and situations that were often completely missed by their elders.

Ike frequently took Charlie with him on weekend jaunts to Camp David, the retreat in Maryland that Eisenhower had named in honor of his father and grandson, both of whom were named David. He liked to bounce ideas off of the young man and hear his comments and suggestions before presenting the complicated problems to his full Cabinet.

On one weekend, their conversation took them back to the war and SHAEF. As their reminiscences turned to the bombing of the mansion in Croydon, Ike asked his trusted advisor if he would consider making a lengthy trip to Britain to speak with several of the generals involved and gain their consent for the president to break the silence about the secret meeting and present much deserved medals to both Charlie and Jack. King George VI had died only months before, and had been succeeded by his oldest daughter, Elizabeth II. Winston Churchill was Prime Minister. He would doubtless give Charlie an audience.

Patton was dead, but Omar Bradley was still alive and kicking, as was General Montgomery, still as pompous and obnoxious as usual. Three other subordinate generals, two of them British, were still active. One of the men in civilian dress the two airmen had dragged from the house was actually French General Charles de Gaulle, leader of the Free French Forces and titular head of the French Resistance throughout the war. He had proved to be invaluable to the Allied forces, both during the D-Day invasion and the subsequent push across France and Germany. De Gaulle was still alive and very active in French politics. Perhaps he would speak with Charlie if Ike called him first.

Three months of travel and negotiation produced a compromise which, as usual, made no one happy. The distinguished group determined that while both American airmen had performed far above and beyond the call of duty, and were certainly deserving of their nation's highest awards, public knowledge of the affair would cause great embarrassment to all of the Allied leaders for the lapse of security that led to the bombardment. Beyond that, there was still considerable antipathy among many of the British, French, and Americans against Germany, and making public the details of a sneak German attack on the bulk of the Allied leaders could cause attacks on the German people at a time that the country was still undergoing massive rebuilding efforts. Public awards for valor were not worth the risk.

The group did agree to allow each country represented at the secret Croydon meeting to make whatever awards to the two soldiers that they saw fit, but the awards would be made to unnamed heroes. No public announcement would ever be made, and the two recipients would never know of the awards they received. It was, as Charlie Bradley said to himself decades later when he heard of Jack's death, one of those classically stupid ideas that could only be conjured up in the minds of politicians.

Over the next several years, Charlie used his international contacts to find out which specific medals had been bestowed, but he never told anyone of either the decorations or the incident that had led to their award. After Ike's retirement in 1961, Charlie was surprised when he was asked to come to England and meet with Prime Minister Harold Macmillan. He had met many dignitaries during his career with President Eisenhower, but never, except for dragging an unconscious Winston Churchill out of a falling building, had he met a Prime Minister. Days later he stood nervously in front of the Minister's desk at Number 10 Downing Street. The great man stared intently at him for a full minute, then arose from his chair, walked around his desk, and shook Charlie's hand.

"Young man, I have heard a great deal about you," he began. Indicating a pair of chairs near his desk, he said, "Please, take a seat. I have a proposition for you."

Charlie was surprised, but sat as requested and remained silent until the Prime Minister was seated beside him. "A proposition, sir?" he finally asked.

The PM smiled, revealing the crooked and stained teeth common to the British working class. "Yes, Mr. Bradley, a proposition. Mr. Churchill and I never really got along, you know."

Charlie didn't, in fact, know that, but he continued to listen.

"Before he stepped down as PM, he and I had a civil conversation in this very office. Eisenhower was mentioned, and your name came up by association. Churchill told me you were the most talented military and political administrator he had ever encountered. 'If he didn't work for Ike,' he told me, 'I would steal him away to work in this office.'" The PM sat back in his chair. "Churchill could be a gruff man, and didn't care whom he offended, but he had a...a 'crackerjack' staff, as you Americans might say. The fact that he wanted you on his staff says more about you than any formal set of credentials or degrees. If Churchill wanted you, then I want you. President Eisenhower has retired to his farm in Gettysburg. You, for all practical purposes, are a young man who is out of a job." He paused for a moment, looking into Charlie's eyes. "I would be pleased if you would come to work for me."

Charlie was stunned, and spent two weeks making his decision. He spoke to Ike on three occasions, and was assured by the recently retired President that it was a great offer.

"You're qualified, Charlie, and Churchill was right...you truly are a great administrator, a great advisor, and you've been a great friend. Please go to England. Sooner or later Mamie and I will tire of farm life, and we'll probably come visit you.

**

Six months after moving to England, Charlie was even more surprised when he was summoned to Buckingham Palace to meet Queen Elizabeth II. The summons was delivered by his boss, Prime Minister Macmillan.

"Her Majesty asked that you accompany me to our regularly scheduled weekly conference this Friday. I will meet with the Queen while you wait in an anteroom. When we are finished, I will retrieve you from the room and introduce you to Her Majesty. After the introduction, I will leave, and she will discuss with you what she will."

"Sir, do you know why the Queen wants to see me?" Charlie asked.

"I have absolutely no idea, Charlie," the PM answered, "but I can tell you this. It has been at least a few decades since a British monarch has ordered a beheading in the public square, so that's probably not something about which you should worry." He laughed as he took a seat at his desk.

On Friday afternoon Charlie stood timidly before Queen Elizabeth II. He was surprised at her age, at least ten years younger than him.

"Please, be seated Mr. Bradley," she said in a friendly tone. When Charlie smiled, the Queen asked, "Do you find something funny, Mr. Bradley?"

Charlie quickly stopped smiling and said, "No, ma'am, that is, Your Highness. I was enjoying your accent. I have always enjoyed the British accent, but I almost always speak with men. It's particularly delightful to hear that accent delivered by a woman...that is, by a Queen...that is..."

Queen Elizabeth was laughing. "It is all right, Mr. Bradley. Don't worry that you will offend me. And thank you for the compliment, although I should remind you that in this country it is *you* who speaks with an accent." She continued to laugh for a moment, putting Charlie completely at ease.

Finally she became serious. Retrieving a white linen envelope from her desk she walked around and sat across from Charlie, a small oval table between them. She laid the envelope on the table. "There is a letter in that envelope that I wrote during the war years when I was a small child. I would like for you to read it."

Charlie extracted the letter and saw a neat cursive script covering the page. He read.

Dear American Soldier,

I do not know your name, but am aware that you are currently being treated at St. Bartholomew's Hospital here in London. I have heard the story from my Papa, who is George VI, King of England, of how you protected him from a falling building by covering him with your own body, receiving great injury to yourself. There is no way I can express proper gratitude to you for saving the life of my dear father. If I were Queen, I would Knight you, but I am just a little girl. Please accept my gratitude, sir, and that of all the People of England.

Elizabeth Windsor

Charlie read the letter three times, finally looking up at Queen Elizabeth. "Jack," he said. "that's his name. He and I grew up together long, long ago. I was with him when the house was crumbling before our eyes. I helped him drag out Churchill, Eisenhower, and others. Finally I was injured and couldn't help any more. Jack crawled in and found King George...only he didn't know it was King George...under a table. As they crawled out, the building collapsed on them, and Jack threw his body over the King's." He looked once more at the Queen and noticed tears in her eyes. "They were actually under the bricks for two days before rescuers reached them. Jack was hospitalized for over two years, but fully recovered. He still lives in America, with three fine children, a lovely wife, and a good life. He doesn't remember the incident at all...has no idea that he saved the King of England."

"Is that why you wanted to see me, Your Highness?" Charlie suddenly asked. "To find out his name?"

"I wanted to give you this letter," the Queen answered, "and to give you another." She stood, prompting Charlie to do so as well, and walked around her desk. She opened a drawer and produced a single sheet of paper. Charlie immediately noticed the Royal seal at the top of the sheet. Elizabeth handed him the paper.

"This letter confers a Knighthood upon your friend, Jack. It is the highest honor England can bestow upon the man who saved the King at the risk of his own life. In your version of the story, your friend did not even know the man he was saving was, in fact, the King. That somehow makes his actions even more admirable, more worthy of a British Knighthood." She indicated the letter on the oval table. "In that letter, which I wrote many years ago, I said I would Knight him if it were in my power. Now it *is* in my power. I only regret I did not do it long ago."

She sat down behind her desk, while Charlie remained standing. "Mr. Bradley, I understand the surviving members of the Croydon bombing have decided you and my father's benefactor can never actually possess the awards you deserve." She handed Bradley the letter of Knighthood, and said, "Please take this and place it in the envelope with the letter I wrote as a child. If ever there is a chance, if ever the generals and world leaders come to their senses and allow you great heroes to be recognized, please give them to your friend with my thanks and my deepest admiration."

"Yes, Your Highness," Charlie answered after a moment's pause. He picked up the letters and stood facing the Queen.

"Thank you for coming, Mr. Bradley," the Queen of England said, dismissing him with a smile.

Chapter 26

March, 2007

Charlie Bradley stared another moment at Jack's coffin, then turned to leave.

"Sir, what about that leather pack?" one of the cemetery attendants asked. "Don't you want to keep it?"

"Just lower it with the coffin," Charlie answered. "That letter is Jack's, not mine. I think it's best we bury it with him." The old man shook his head in disgust. Here to be buried was a man who saved Dwight Eisenhower, Winston Churchill, Omar Bradley, General Sir Bernard Montgomery, Charles de Gaulle, the King of England, and several more of the architects of the D-Day Invasion. Had chance not brought Jack to Croydon at just the right time, those men would likely have been killed, the invasion plans abandoned, and England would quickly have been overrun by the Nazis in the leaderless chaos that would have followed. Jack had saved Europe. His selfless action had, for all practical purposes, won the war.

"Yes, sir," answered the attendant. "We will do just that. We'll bury it with the coffin."

Charlie walked away, turning to look back one last time as he reached the top of the knoll. It was a great story, he thought. Too bad no one would ever know.

**

In a small cemetery in southern Missouri is a black granite headstone over the grave of a man named Jack. On the back of the stone is attached the standard bronze marker issued by the Department of Veterans Affairs to those who have served their country in the United States Military. The bronze plaque was not originally part of the headstone.

At some point in time, some unknown person attached three military medals to the back of the black stone...the French Legion of Honor, the British Victoria Cross, and America's highest honor, the Medal of Honor.

Only a few days later, before anyone noticed the medals, government agents slipped into the cemetery and chipped the medals away with a hammer and chisel. No one was ever to know what this man had done. To hide the roughened area where they had defaced the headstone, the agents attached the bronze marker denoting Jack's military service. They had no way to know that beneath their feet lay what was perhaps the highest possible honor bestowed upon the selfless, unknown hero who lay in the coffin...Sir Jack.

Author's Notes

My dad, whose name just happened to be Jack, like that of the protagonist in my story, was a veteran of World War II. Like many of his generation, he volunteered to go to war, did his job, and came home to resume his civilian life with no criticism of the Army or his government, no boasting of what he did 'over there,' and no complaints about the physical or emotional wounds received from battle and the horrors of war. As I was growing up, Dad never told stories of what he did in the war. I remember as a child standing in front of his old uniform, which was hung in a corner of our dank basement along with other old and used up clothing, and wondering what he did to receive those ribbons that were displayed on the jacket. When I asked about the medals or his wartime activities, he would only smile and say something like, "I don't even remember, son. That was a long time ago, and it's not part of my life anymore."

In 1998 I was flying Dad down to Florida for some deep sea fishing on his seventy-fifth birthday. The single engine of our light plane conked out right over the Florida-Alabama state line, and we crash landed into a very small field bounded on all sides by pine forest. We touched down at about a hundred mph with a stiff tailwind, bounced off of a couple trees, and crashed through a fence before finally grinding to a stop. After crawling out the door and ascertaining that we had no significant injuries, Dad surveyed the sky for a long time before finally saying, "Well, at least there aren't any Germans up there this time."

My mind immediately went back to that uniform and those ribbons, but I didn't ask the obvious question. I already knew what the answer would be. There was very likely a great story there that I would never hear. The incident did, however, give me the idea to write this story. I have tossed it around for over a decade while writing other books that actually held less interest for me. Finally, after much research of military records, internet blogs, and discussions with Dad's acquaintances who knew a little of his military service, I pieced together the initial seeds of a story.

Unspoken Valor is fiction, but there is a great deal of factual information within its pages.

**

The Campbell Chicks were, in fact, a semi-professional baseball team in the years before WWII. Similar teams abounded across the nation, providing entertainment and even local heroes for residents of small towns before the era of television and readily accessible entertainment. Dad played for the Chicks, and, while not a power hitter, was known for his ability to place his hits through holes in the defense, enabling him to maintain a three hundred plus batting average.

The Chicks lost many players to WWII, but most returned safely home after the war.

**

The 925th Engineer Aviation Regiment came into existence on July 2, 1943 at March Field, California, pretty much as was described in the book. After only a month of breakneck training, a mountain of paperwork (in triplicate, of course), and hectic preparation, the 925th shipped out by train to their staging area at Camp Kilmer, New Jersey. After more frantic preparation and overcoming a few equipment and personnel snafus, the group shipped out on the HMS Queen Elizabeth on August 20, 1943. Dad was part of the 925th from day one.

**

Dad and his buddies were able to go into New York City on August 17 and watch his favorite team, the St. Louis Cardinals defeat the Brooklyn Dodgers 7-3. I can remember only two stories Dad ever told me about his experiences in the Army Air Corps, and both of them had to do with baseball.

—-+--— —+- — —+- — — +- — —+- — —+- — —+- — —+- — —+- — — +- — —+- — —+- — —-+--

**

The Regiment arrived in Gourock, Scotland and traveled by train to Boreham, England, a tiny hamlet just a few miles from Chelmsford, where they were tasked to build an air strip for bombing operations against Germany. The young men of the 925th, most of whom had never been outside the United States were introduced to Brussel sprouts, Spam, and Bitters. They were taught to erect a new kind of barracks called Nissen Huts, which would become their homes after completion.

**

Jack Abernathy and one other man were listed as the first casualties of the 925th on December 23, 1943. Records of the event were sketchy and incomplete, but Jack's injuries were incurred in an area west of London rather than on base at Boreham, which was east of the city. Private Abernathy sustained serious injuries to his head and both legs, and did, in fact, have amnesia throughout the Twelve Days of Christmas in 1943-44. Doctors and friends reported visiting him in a London hospital, finding him talkative and in good spirits, but floating in and out of awareness of his current situation. Throughout the remainder of his life, he remembered none of it.

**

The story about bombing the Chicago Cubs in their dugout was never reported in any newspapers, so probably never happened. It was, however, related to me by my father while he was in a hospital recovery room waking up from a surgical procedure, and I consider it to be one of his rare 'war stories'. While doubtless the product of, shall we say, over medication, it was a great story deserving of being recorded for posterity.

**

The sections in which I described the extreme discomfort and terror faced by the B-17 crews was taken from reports and blogs by actual combatants. My poor attempts at portrayal of the dread and horror faced by the brave men who manned the bombers cannot begin to be descriptive of the actual facts. These brave crews fought valiantly in conditions that are unimaginable to most of us. Casualties were high, and those who survived being shot down often were treated reprehensibly in German prison camps until the war ended. They were truly heroes at an order of magnitude that defies literary description.

**

During the time I was researching the horrors of war faced by B-17 crews, I was privileged and honored to be allowed to fly in a B-17 owned and maintained by the Experimental Aircraft Association. Named "Aluminum Overcast," the craft is still a magnificent war bird that flies throughout the nation as a traveling museum. I was able to sit in the pilot's seat, climb into the turret where the flight engineer fired his twin guns and oversaw the health of the aircraft, and sit in the Plexiglas nose, with its magnificent view, where the bombardier and navigator served during flight. Tears welled in my eyes when I stood in the port waist gun position (my dad's crew position) and moved the fifty caliber machine gun around at imaginary targets. I could imagine being surrounded by a squadron of aircraft in Javelin Down formation. I could even imagine enemy fighters darting in and out of the formation. Try as I might, however, I could not even begin to imagine the terror of the crewmen, many of whom were not yet twenty years old, or the bravery that held them together. The flight for me was a wonderful but humbling experience.

**

The episode describing Lieutenant John C. Morgan bringing in his B-17 with a seriously injured and mentally unstable pilot, whom he had to fight off with one hand while flying the crippled aircraft with the other, was factual. Lietuenant Morgan was awarded the Medal of Honor for his brave actions.

—·—— —·—— —·— —·— —·— —·—— —·——— —·— —·—— —·— ——·——

**

Many of the episodes involving Generals Eisenhower, Smith, Montgomery, and Patton, were fictional accounts, but I endeavored to present all of those actual characters in a manner that reflected their personalities and command styles. General George Patton was, in fact, set up as a decoy in charge of an elaborate make-believe army designed to mislead the German Army into believing what would be the D-Day Invasion would be against Calais rather than Normandy.

**

Admiral Wilhelm Canaris was head of the Abwer, or German intelligence organization before and during World War II. He was a decorated submariner during the first world war, and loved Germany every bit as much as he despised Hitler, Himmler, and the Nazi Reich. He was every bit the enigma I presented him to be...to both sides. More than once in his career, Canaris was part of plans to assassinate Hitler. At the same time, Der Fuehrer had heard rumors of plots against his life, and ordered Canaris to find those responsible. Remarkably, the Admiral ferreted out several officers involved in various assassination plots and turned them over to Hitler while actively plotting with his own group. His role in the plot to eliminate Hitler was finally discovered, and Canaris was hanged, along with several other conspirators, during the last few days of the war. His final words were, "I die for my fatherland. I have a clear conscience. I only did my duty to my country when I tried to oppose the criminal folly of Hitler."

**

As I mentioned earlier in the book, my father never talked about his military service, so I do not know the actual name of the B-17 in which he crewed. It definitely was not "Hitler's Headache," for that particular aircraft was not flown until later in the war. The real "Hitler's Headache" was a B-17 tasked to bomb the Nazi Reich, so I took the liberty of using it for my story. The photograph of the aircraft was taken from the website 398th.org, which is maintained by the 398th Bomb Group Memorial Association. There are several photos on the site, including that of "Hitler's Headache," in which the crews have never been identified. If you happen to see someone in the photo that you recognize, I'm certain the association would be very appreciative of any information you can provide.

**

Active until his last few days, Dad died in March, 2007. His burial in the small cemetery in Campbell, Missouri was pretty much as described. A U.S. Air Force honor guard and a lone bagpiper were part of the graveside service. Many of the mourners, including myself, still have no idea why the actual Air Force honor guard was in attendance rather than the usual group from the local VFW. Dad has a black granite headstone, as described. On the back of the stone is a bronze plaque similar to those seen throughout the United States denoting the military service of the interred. The plaque was not attached until several days after the headstone was placed. There are those who say the stone had a marred surface, as if it had been scarred with a chisel, in the area hidden by the plaque.

**

Those, along with a few others unmentioned, are the facts. The rest of the story is comprised of supposition, guesswork, and a fair amount of unabashed fiction. If I did my job well, you should never know exactly where I have crossed the line from truth to other-than-truth.

Dad may or may not have single-handedly won World War II, but it is the prerogative of a son to idolize his father and look to him as his greatest hero. My father's misfortune, I suppose, was to have a son who became a writer, and would put his story down on paper. Dad would never have told this story, even the factual parts of it, because that was not his way. I hope I have done him some justice by telling it exactly the way I hope it happened.

**

One more bit of factual information: You *can* find dry wood and kindling even in a soaking rain...if you know where to look.

Photo donated to the 398th Bomb Group by Norman Taylor. "Hitler's Headache" was first assigned on Feb. 7, 1945. After flying 23 missions it returned to the United States on May 21, 1945. This photograph was taken on its return to Bradley Field, Connecticut. Crew members in this picture are all unidentified.

This photograph, along with many others, is maintained on the website of the 398th Bomb Group Memorial Association. If you can identify any of the crewmen above, please contact the association at crewpictures@398th.org.

Photo used with permission from the 398th Association and Norman Taylor.

B-17s grouped in combat boxes (above) in 1943.

A tough and resilient aircraft, B-17's often returned with injured crews flying machines with extreme damage. Somehow they made it home.

Admiral Wilhelm Canaris (above) was involved in plots to assassinate Hitler.

Fake airplanes constructed of canvas and wood, such as the one above, were used to deceive enemy reconnaissance aircraft.

Winston Churchill (above) was Prime Minister of the United Kingdom 1940-1945 and 1951-1955.

HMS Achilles was a Warrior-class armored cruiser that served throughout the First World War.

Slugger Joe DiMaggio gave up his nearly $50K annual baseball salary for $50 per month Army pay in 1943-1945.

St. Louis Cardinal great Stan Musial missed the 1945 baseball season while serving in the Navy. Here, Stan the Man is awarded the Medal of Freedom in 2011.

King George VI

Painting of seven-year-old Princess Elizabeth

On their arrival in Borham, England the first order of business was to construct Nissen Huts (above) to serve as troop quarters, hospital, and administrative buildings. C-rations (below) made up most of the troops' meals until a kitchen/mess hall was built. Notice the P-38 can opener on the C-ration can on the right.

Lieutenant John C. Morgan was awarded the Medal of Honor for saving his crew by landing a seriously crippled B-17 while wounded and fighting off his pilot, who was crazed from a head wound. Morgan was shot down and captured in March 1944 and spent the remainder of the war in a POW camp.

General Curtis LeMay (above) designed the combat box formation known as 'Javelin Down' (below) as a way for bomber groups to defend themselves with maximum firepower against the enemy.

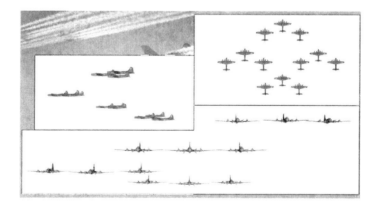

Lockheed P-38 Lightning, known as the Fork-Tailed Devil by the German Luftwaffe for its maneuverability and destructive capabilities.

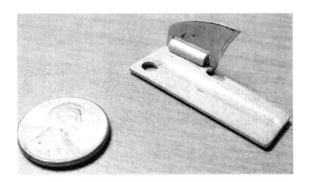

The P-38 can opener was developed in 1942 to open K-ration and C-ration cans. The name came from the fact that it took 38 punctures to open the can by "walking" the blade around it.

The Sullivan brothers (above) enlisted in the Navy on January 3, 1942 with the stipulation that they all serve together. They were all assigned to the light cruiser USS Juneau, and were killed in action when the Juneau (below) was sunk on November 13, 1942.
From left to right: Joseph, Francis, Albert, Madison, and George.

General Dwight Eisenhower was Supreme Commander of Allied forces during WWII.

SHAEF commanders left to right: General Bradley, Admiral Ramsay, Air Marshall Tedder, General Eisenhower, General Montgomery, Air Marshall Leigh-Mallory, General Smith

*Photos and descriptions courtesy of Wiki Commons

Steven Abernathy was first published in 1973 while writing educational materials for ESP., Inc. He was educated at the United State Air Force Academy, Arkansas State University, and the University of Tennessee.

The author has had a variety of life experiences, all of which he credits as contributors to his writing style. "I have worked as a farm laborer, truck driver, carpenter, and door-to-door salesman. I have been a military officer, a public school teacher, a dentist, and a newspaper columnist. I have survived a heart attack, an airplane crash, and a race as candidate for U. S. Congress. I have shared a bologna sandwich with fellow farm laborers while relaxing under a wagon, and have dined more formally with Bill Clinton. Once I even had lunch with Connie Kreski (Playboy Playmate of the Year in 1969.) She was infinitely more interesting than President Clinton," he quips.

Steven lives in Destin, Florida and Jonesboro, Arkansas with his lovely wife of 41 years, Michele. *Unspoken Valor"* is the author's fourth novel.

CPSIA information can be obtained at www.ICGtesting.com
Printed in the USA
LVOW07s0605031114

411664LV00003B/5/P